THE GIRLS OF OLD EDEN SCHOOL

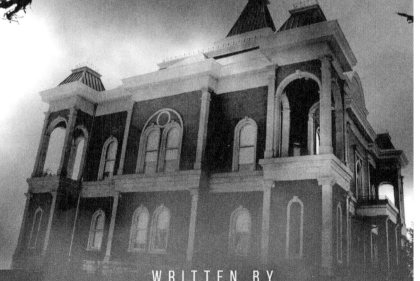

WRITTEN BY

BRIANNA RAINE

The Girls of Old Eden School
By Brianna Raine

Question Mark Press

Published 2023 by Question Mark Horror

Copyright by Question Mark Horror/Brianna Raine

This is a work of fiction. Names, characters, places, and incidents are a product of the author's imagination. Locales and public names are sometimes used for atmospheric purposes. Any resemblance to actual people, living or dead, or to businesses, companies, events, institutions or locales is completely coincidental.

The Girls Of Old Eden School - 1st Edition

For my grandad, Mike Reynolds, who has continued to support me on my writing journey since day one and for having faith in me. Love you Grandad.

Acknowledgements

Thanks you to my friends and family who have been supportive of me throughout the writing of The Girls of Old Eden School. I also thank Question Mark Press for their continued help and support when I have needed their help, especially to Jim Ody and the editors and beta readers.

Special thanks to my team of ARC readers for taking time out of their days to read my book before sending to print, you were all a major help!

And finally, to you my readers for choosing to purchase this book. I hope you enjoy it.

Edited by Sue Scott & Heather Ann Larson.
Beta read by Tasha Schied.

PROLOGUE

ABIGAIL WOKE UP TO FIND HER staring at her from the foot of her bed, with her hand held out towards her, as if encouraging Abigail to go with her.

Abigail played with the little girl in between classes and after dinner out in the gardens, or when the weather was not in their favour, they would hide out in the attic, away from everyone else.

Failing to fit in at school, she didn't have any friends. Everyone else was there because their parents were wealthy and wanted them to have the best education. But not hers.

Abigail's mum had gained the insurance money from her husband's death and used it to ship her to this God-forsaken school, while she made a new family with Brian. Brian didn't like Abigail and wanted, more than anything, for her to be out of the way. He got his wish. It didn't help that her mum wanted her gone, too, but for an entirely different reason. She was just a reminder of her father. Every time she looked at Abigail it brought back so much pain. It got to the point where she couldn't even gaze upon Abigail any longer, so she sent her as far away as she possibly could. And this was something that wasn't lost on the other kids.

Instead of taking pity on the poor child, they would bully her and tell her she was not wanted there, the same way her mother had.

That was when Sylvie came along. She understood the feeling of being unwanted and pushed aside. She was, after all, abandoned on the steps of the orphanage as a baby. She wanted Abigail to feel better. She wanted to be her friend. She didn't want her to be lonely anymore, so she played with her whenever she could.

One night, Sylvie heard her crying in her sleep, so she went to comfort her. She wanted more than anything to help her. Abigail was startled awake to find Sylvie, cloaked by the darkness and at the end of her bed, holding out her hand.

"Come with me," Sylvie whispered. "I have something to show you."

Wearing only her long white nightdress, she wiped the sleep from her eyes and climbed clumsily out of her bed. She followed Sylvie out of the dorm and into the hall. The rest of the girls remained asleep as she crept out of the room.

They went to their usual hiding space, the attic. Up there, they could talk in private and no one would ever find them. The attic was full of broken furniture, dusty piles of books, and boxes upon boxes of old work by the students, including canvas paintings and sculptures.

They had made a space between the tall, metal shelving units full of art supplies. They placed a couple of old cushions and had thrown a blanket over them to create a small seating area, adding a small lamp beside it for light.

There was something up there Abigail was unaware of though. Little did she realise she was about to find out what was really keeping Sylvie here.

Sylvie led her to the other end of the attic, past their comfy little hideaway and the safety of the old lamp. That end of the attic was in complete darkness, the small lamp's light unable to reach into its dreary depths. There were no sockets at that end of the attic, so there were no options for light sources, and she had

2

no access to a torch. The light from the cosy area she had made up acted as an invitation to go back, not to keep heading into the gloom before her.

"What are we doing, Sylvie?" Abigail questioned. She could feel the nerves crackle in her throat as she asked.

"I want you to be happy, Abigail. I can take all that pain away for you. You won't ever have to worry about those bullies ever again. We can be friends forever. My other friends will love you, as well."

"How?" not quite sure she really wanted to ask; nevertheless, the words escaped her lips before she had the chance to stop them.

"Here." Sylvie opened a little wooden door. A gush of cold wind came in. The sensation was like tiny shards of ice hitting Abigail's skin. The small door led to the outside. Abigail could see a single wooden beam jolting out from the small opening and into the cold night air.

It was as if the beam led her to the glittering stars in the night sky. She felt mesmerised by their twinkling. A calmness came over her. The anxiety she had felt fluttering in her stomach had gone, leaving her feeling as light as a cloud.

Sylvie took Abigail's hands in hers and gently walked out onto the beam. Abigail's eyes were focused directly on the stars above her, almost like she was in a sleepy trance. She continued to step forward, one foot slowly after the other, without even thinking about it, until there was no beam left to tread.

A high-pitched scream filled the dark atmosphere around Old Eden School.

CHAPTER
ONE
MISS HART

JENNY HART HAD A TROUBLING SUMMER. Just before the holidays even started, the local school where she'd been working dropped some devastating news. Along with other members of staff, she'd been made redundant.

She loved her job working with the young children and had worked hard to get to where she was. She had started out as a teaching assistant and had studied hard to finally become a teacher at the same school.

The last day of school was upsetting, to say the least, having to say goodbye to the children and the friends she'd made during her time there over the last four years. Even the children were crying and giving her hugs at the school gate as they left for the holidays.

She would always remember the children, some more than others. Little Henry was one of them. He had bright orange hair and freckles that smothered his face. He was fond of Jenny and would always ask for her help with absolutely anything he could think of. Tying his shoelaces. Spelling a particular word he struggled with all the time and whenever she explained it to him, he would giggle his little heart out.

"Big elephants cause accidents under small elephants," he'd chuckle. He would imagine mummy and daddy elephants leaving

4

hot steaming poops all over the place and the baby elephant stepping into them. *Oh, the thoughts of little boys!*

Then there was Emily. Such a pretty little girl. Her blonde hair was always tied neatly in braids with little blue bows at the ends. The only thing not nice and neat was her nose. It was always dripping with snot, little slimy slithers running from her nostrils to the top of her lips. Regardless of the children's funny-or disgusting-little quirks, they were well-behaved and always having fun.

It was a half day, as it was the last day before the summer, meaning Miss Hart finished at one pm and the children at twelve pm.

It was twelve forty-five, and she started to gather up all the gifts she had been given by both the children and her co-workers. Boxes of chocolates, bath bombs, flowers, a *Best Teacher* mug with matching keyring, and even a handmade card signed by all the children in her class. As she read it, tears welled up in her eyes, threatening to escape and run away down her cheeks. She was going to miss so much about this job.

We will never forget you, Miss. You will always be my favourite teacher. You're the best. Don't forget us.

So many messages. She would never forget the school or the lovely children she taught.

"Pull yourself together, woman," she whispered to herself, squeezing her eyes tight and wiping the back of her hand over both eyes before scooping all the items up into her arms and heading to her car.

When she got home, her fiancé's car was already sitting on the driveway. She started to feel a bit happier. He must have taken the afternoon off, knowing it was her last day and she would need some comforting. He was often thoughtful like that. Whenever she needed a bit of cheering up, he was there. He would cook her special meals and buy her little treats. It didn't have to be anything big and fancy, just something to either make her smile or make her laugh so she forgot about whatever it was that was getting her down.

She opened the front door and placed her box full of gifts on the table in the hallway and her keys in the small bowl. She looked up into the mirror, noticed the mascara traces on her cheeks, and quickly licked her finger and rubbed the tear marks away. Whilst she looked better, the residual sadness remained.

She headed into the kitchen and saw a bottle of wine with two glasses already poured and a bunch of flowers sitting in a glass vase on the side. There was a little envelope placed amongst the flowers. With a small smile, she pinched the envelope from its plastic holder and read the small card inside. *We have a job proposal for you here at Old Eden School. Give us a call.*

She had expected the flowers to be from her fiancé. How did another school know she was in need of a job? She hadn't even applied for anything yet or let any employment agencies know she was on the search. She had never even heard of Old Eden School.

She took out her phone and started to look up Old Eden School. As she typed into her phone, she made her way up the stairs and into her fiancé's office. She pushed the door open and made her way in to tell him about the flowers and job opportunity.

"Hey darling, the weirdest thing…" But before she could continue her sentence, she looked up. There before her stood her fiancé, completely naked, thrusting into another woman who lay upon his desk. Paperwork was scattered across the room and their clothes had been flung all over the floor in the whirlwind of lust.

Her words held captive in her throat as the vision before her made bile rise from her stomach.

They hadn't been that intimate in months! The last time he had her in his grasp like that was after a night of heavy drinking at his work's Christmas do. His hands rubbed over her breasts and pinched her rosy nipples as he had her bent over his desk. He had even ripped her sparkling blue dress right down the middle, causing her to gasp in excitement beforehand. But now, he was with *her*. She wasn't even pretty! Slim, yes. Young, yes. But pretty, not to her. Dark, thin hair. Crooked nose. Even HE had commented on her nose at the Christmas party! *Was he just saying that to cover up any feelings he had for her?*

The thoughts of their last passionate night together were now dirtied in her mind as she gazed up at the woman beneath her fiancé. Jenny recognised her the moment her eyes opened post-orgasm. It was such a damned cliché. *His bloody assistant! Really?*

"What... the fuck?" She finally got her words to form, but as they came out, they were broken as she tried not to cry.

"SHIT!" he exclaimed, pulling away from the other woman and rushing to get his clothes. He had completely forgotten that it was Jenny's last day and that she would be finishing early.

"Jenny! I'm so sorry."

Her eyes were frozen, glued to the floor where paperwork and pens lay scattered in a mess. She started to back away slowly.

It was as if she were stuck in a snow globe, but it wasn't snow falling around her; it was her whole life. Everything she had planned! Their wedding, saving up for when they start a family, all of it came crashing down around her in a single moment. She had just lost her job, and now this!

"Jenny, wait! Please wait!" he called out.

Jenny had turned away in disgust and started making her way down the stairs, holding onto the railing for support. A lump formed in her throat, making it hard for her to breathe. She couldn't collapse here, not with him and *HER* upstairs. She needed to get away.

"Jen please!" He buttoned up his trousers and ran after Jenny to grab her arm, begging her to talk to him.

"Get your filthy hands off me! How fucking dare you! You don't ever get to touch me again." She whipped her arm away from him in anger.

She grabbed the note from the flowers, stormed through the hallway, grabbed her keys and handbag, and shot out of the door without another word to him.

She had no spare clothes, none of her belongings. Where would she even go? Her mother lived on her own thirty miles away, she didn't really have many friends, and the one she could rely on was already on her way to the airport to start her holiday.

After speeding off away from the house, she pulled up on the side of the road and burst into tears. The tears she had held in so she could focus on the road. They came flooding out as soon as she turned the key in the ignition. Her head fell forward on the steering wheel, and she screamed in grief with her arms covering her head.

They had so many memories together and her mind was playing them on a loop. Her life felt like it no longer had meaning. The times they would sit on the sofa and talk about the children they would have together, a boy and a girl. James and Ruby. They would have a boy first so that he could look after his little sister, of course, all the while knowing they obviously couldn't pick and choose. But it was their fantasy. Their dream. Their future.

Then there was the night he asked her to marry him. It was mid-July the year before. He had prepared a candlelit dinner on a private yacht. The sun was setting. The sky was painted in pinks, oranges, and reds. A warm breeze drifted between them as they fed each other pudding. She had a chocolate sponge with raspberries and a white chocolate sauce, and he had the creamiest cheesecake she had ever tasted. Not waiting any longer, he placed his fork down after placing a small piece of dessert in her mouth and knelt on one knee. The timing completely surprised her. She had been expecting the question, just not mid-mouthful.

Later, when they'd made love, she'd felt complete. Like now they were a couple forever. He'd held her naked in his arms and she'd fallen to sleep smiling and content.

Looking back on her memory of this made her laugh before. But now, it hurt more than anything she had felt before. She needed to let it all out, and she felt better for doing so.

Pulling her head up and wiping away the tears that had soaked her face, her eyes searched for her bag. Grabbing it from the foot well on the passenger side and placing it on her tear-soaked lap, she dragged out her phone to call her mum. Just the thought of calling her caused the next round of tears to invade her eyes, but as she pulled out her phone, a small bottle of pills rolled out, along with the small card from the flowers, and fell between her feet.

She stopped what she was doing to gain focus. She took a deep breath in through her nose and slowly out through her mouth. She now had a choice, and this was a difficult one for her. Memories of bad habits from another lifetime came flooding into her mind as she held the small plastic bottle.

That was a time she felt unworthy of love. A time when her father used to beat her to a pulp, leaving her black and blue. Her mum had divorced him but was unable to take Jenny with her. She was left with an alcoholic father who showed her no kindness and forced her to work to pay their bills, and, most importantly, his drink. It got to a point that when he passed out on the sofa, she would rummage through the medicine cabinet in the bathroom. Anything to feel numb, stop her feeling the pain deep inside.

Her dad, suffering from bad hangovers the morning after an alcohol binge, would always have a couple of bottles worth of painkillers stashed away in the cupboard. She wanted more than anything for her pain to be gone. Her physical pain. Her emotional pain. And the pills did just that. She would pop a couple onto the side of the sink, and with a small spoon that she used to keep hidden between the face cloths would crush them into a powder, lower her face, and snort the substance into her nose. She didn't mean for it to become a habit, but nothing else helped to rid her pain.

Her final encounter with substance abuse placed her in the hospital when she turned twenty-one. With no one to love her and help celebrate her life, she overdosed. She didn't even count the number of tablets. She crushed a few and sucked them up her nostrils. She emptied the rest of the pills from the bottle into her hand and didn't think a thing of it. She was numb. Without a thought in her head, she chucked the tablets in her mouth and swallowed. Now she just had to wait. She slumped against the toilet and waited for the darkness to take over.

She was lucky her dad needed the toilet. Pushing the door open and stumbling in holding his throbbing head, he found her there just as her eyes started to roll back in her head. He sobered up quicker than he ever thought possible and rushed in, stuck his fingers deep into her throat, causing her to vomit.

That was the only memory of her dad where he seemed to actually care about her. After that night, she was taken in by her mum for a short time while she studied to become a teacher, reaching as best as she could for the right tracks in life to follow.

All these memories caused her to throw the bottle in the back seat, and she thought of the small card instead. She focused on her breathing for a moment. Slowly, she inhaled in and then out to steady herself. She did this a few times until she was a little calmer. Her breath now steady and eyes clear of tears, she reached into the foot well and grabbed the card.

She never got to look at the results from when she typed in Old Eden School. She placed the card on her lap and opened her phone. On the screen were several different links to choose from. The second one down showed a link to the School's website. She clicked it.

Old Eden School for Girls.

The web page showed a private school for girls, a boarding school where both the children and staff lived on-site. There was also an advertisement for an art teacher and counsellor.

"This must be the position they're asking me to fill," she muttered to herself. "Typical that it comes along when this shit happens." She sighed. She was obviously very keen to take the job, especially as it came with her own room. But where was this place? She looked at the location on Google maps.

Old Eden School, Lower Mourneborough.

"Well," she started, looking at the little red marker on the map, "at least it's in the middle of nowhere."

And it was. It was about an hour and a half's drive away, in the middle of the countryside and surrounded by woodland. She couldn't even see a village or small town nearby. At least being in the middle of nowhere meant her idiotic ex-fiancé couldn't find her. *That's even if he did want to find me. What if he was glad he got caught? Now he could sleep with whomever he wanted without worrying about it. I'm not in the way anymore.*

Tears started to prick at her eyes, but before they even had a chance of falling, she wiped them away. *No! This man doesn't deserve to make you cry. You are better than this, Jenny! You've got this!*

She picked up the card and tapped the phone number into her phone. She didn't waste one more second. She wanted to get away and get away fast. But was this really the best option? A school she had never heard of… in a place she had never heard of… that somehow already knew she was in need of a new job… and just happened to be a live on-site teaching position…

She was certainly going to find out.

CHAPTER TWO
NEW START

JENNY WAS ALMOST THERE. She had called the school and informed them of her situation. Surprisingly, they had invited her straight away, no questions asked.

The journey felt so long, and she was mentally exhausted by the time she got there. After driving along the bypass and main roads around and through small, quaint towns, she had happened upon an old country lane. The dirt track was dry; the tyres sent up clouds of dust into the air as she continued down the lane. It seemed to go on forever, but she didn't mind too much. The trees surrounding the track were the most vivid green, and the sunlight flickered between the leaves in the warm summer breeze. Beyond the trees were lush fields, some with fruitful crops and others with sheep dotted on the rolling hills.

The warm breeze that came flowing through the window, and the quietness of the surroundings, seemed to calm her nerves. After all the stress and whirlwind of events that had happened that day, for just a small moment she felt almost relaxed. Almost.

The road became bumpier, and she realised it had turned into gravel. Up ahead, the sun was starting to set. Its beams were flowing through the gaps of the large iron gate at the end of the road. Next to the entrance was a dominating and slightly weathered wooden sign which read *Old Eden School for Girls*. It had definitely seen better days and was in need of replacing, especially since some little scrotum had sprayed the word *Whores* over where it was supposed to say Girls.

She pulled up in front of the gate and lifted her hand to shade her eyes from the sun streaming in through her window. She pushed the buzzer on the iron entrance. Nothing happened. She buzzed again and the gate started to creak open with a high-pitched, mechanical whine. As it slowly swung inwards, it revealed the long driveway to the school. Jenny lightly pressed the accelerator and crept down the driveway to the school towering over her.

It was huge! She had thought it would be a big school considering it was a boarding school for girls, but this was something else. It sat on its own bank, wild flower beds along the front of the property and to the edge of the steps leading to the entrance. The building itself was old and tired. Looking up at it, you could imagine people from centuries past, walking the corridors or standing on the balcony of one of the towers overlooking the grounds.

Why did she feel like someone was watching her as she pulled up? She opened the car door and looked up at one of the windows on the top floor to see a girl gazing back at her. She had a blank expression as she watched Jenny walk towards the steps, her eyes fixed on her with a stony stare.

"You must be Miss Jenny Hart! I'm Lenora May, Headmistress," a happy voice boomed, making her jump. Lenora stood at the top of the steps in front of the main entrance. She was small in stature, her curly brown hair peppered with silver, although she didn't have one wrinkle on her face. Her blue eyes twinkled in the sunlight.

"Yes. Nice to meet you. I'm so thankful for you reaching out to me. It really couldn't have come at a better time," she replied, shaking Lenora's hand. She looked back up to the window, but the little girl was gone.

"How was your drive? I know the roads around here can be filled with potholes, and getting stuck behind the odd farmer can be such a pain."

"Oh, they were fine. The countryside is lovely, especially with the sun beaming down. It's such a beautiful location."

"It is. Here, let me show you around. The school can be just as lovely at times," Lenora gestured with a warm smile, inviting Jenny in.

Stepping inside the entrance, she walked past a young lady who must have been about sixteen dusting down the windows beside the door. She gave the girl a small grin. The temperature inside was cold, surprising as it was summer and the outside air was beautifully warm. The chill was enough to make her shiver and the hairs on her arms stand up on end.

"Sorry about the coldness in here. We don't get much sun in some parts of the building. It does mean, though, that when it's really hot, at least we can keep cool inside."

"That's okay. Nothing a cardigan won't fix." She smiled as she rubbed her arms to warm them.

"So, on the ground floor, you'll find all the classrooms. I'll show you to yours in a moment. At the end of the building is the hall where meals are served. That's also where you'll find access to the gardens and sports grounds. We have the dorms up on the first floor, along with staff quarters." Jenny found her tone to be strict, but whenever she faced her, she seemed kind. Her appearance was soft. She couldn't quite figure her out.

Jenny used to believe herself a good judge of character, but obviously with her fiancé cheating, she was starting to second guess herself. She wasn't sure at all what to make of her yet. At least the job came with housing. She never really had much time to be worried about it, as everything happened one sequence after another in a very rapid manner. She was thankful it was something she needn't worry about.

They continued along the corridor until they came to an empty classroom.

"This will be your class," Lenora said, opening the door to the classroom.

It was an art room. Student's paintings lined the walls, paint pots were stacked along the bench at the back of the room, and the wooden tables were stained with years' worth of paint splatters. They were almost an art design themselves.

"I hope this meets your standards?" she asked.

"It's huge! My last classroom was a lot smaller, but I'm sure I'll get used to it. How many children will I be teaching?"

"Well, we've had a bit of a reduction in students recently. Unfortunately, one of our girls went missing. It's been two months now. It hit the local papers, and parents pulled their kids from the school. So currently, you have fifteen students."

"Oh…" Jenny knew exactly what she wanted to ask, but how?

"Without wanting to sound rude, is this the only time it's happened? The missing child, I mean?"

"This building is very old and has many stories, as do most of the properties in this area. People going missing, mysterious deaths. It's not unheard of at all and is more disappointing these days rather than surprising."

"So this is a regular occurrence?" Jenny started to wonder whether it was a mistake coming here. Lenora seemed very dismissive that missing children would be deemed a problem. She acted as though it was completely normal.

"No, but maybe once a year. In total, we've had fifteen either dead or missing." Again, no change in her voice. Just direct and to the point. It was as though there was no emotion behind her words at all. As though it didn't matter.

"Oh, is that not strange to you?"

"There's been stranger," she started. "Two years ago, a girl disappeared and was found a few days later on the steps to the entrance, in her nightgown, her face and clothing covered in dry mud and with sticks in her hair. She had no memory of what happened to her but had weird dreams every night that a man was trying to take her. She ended up having to go to the hospital to get help with her mental health. She's being well looked after now."

"Oh, poor thing," Jenny sighed.

"These girls really need someone like you. Yes, someone to teach them, but also someone they can speak to. Someone they feel is approachable."

"I'll do all I can."

Lenora smiled approvingly at her and led Jenny out of the Art room and towards the large staircase.

"Let me show you to your room."

The staircase was an old, dark walnut, which really could use a clean and polish. As she climbed the carpeted steps, her hand glided up the banister, and as she reached the top, she noticed the thick dust falling from her hand onto the floor.

"I'm so sorry about the dust. Our cleaner has had a week off. She's back tomorrow, though."

"Oh, was that not her downstairs?" Jenny asked, remembering the lady dusting the windows.

"Who, dear? I didn't see anyone." Lenora acted confused.

"The young lady by the front door?" she questioned as she was led into her room.

"Jenny, are you feeling okay? I know today has been very stressful for you. Maybe it's all been a bit too much for you. Stress can do a lot to us physically and mentally. Why don't you get settled in and have a nap? Dinner is at six pm, and tomorrow I will take you shopping. I'll give you a small advance so you can get settled and have the things you need."

Jenny stood with a confused look across her face. Did she imagine her? It *had* been a stressful day and a lot had happened. She had tried to push her fiancé's cheating out of her mind and just focus on her new job opportunity, but now that she was in her new room, on her own with no possessions, she could think of nothing but him and his... *ugh*... mistress. Just the thought of them made her stomach twist and turn into knots. She ran to her en-suite as fast as she could and threw up into the toilet bowl.

How was she meant to eat in a few hours? She was so nauseous and really not in the mood to meet everyone this evening, but it would be rude to just not turn up, especially since they had given her this opportunity and allowed her to start straight away. She would be homeless if it weren't for them.

She dragged herself back into her room, laid on her bed, and closed her eyes. She embraced herself in a sad hug trying to comfort herself. A little nap would make her feel better. After a bit of rest, she would feel more energised and ready to meet everyone.

CHAPTER THREE
MEETING MR HUGHES

SHE DREAMED.

A row of children lined the narrow hallway at the bottom of the stairs. They looked to be dressed in their Sunday best, and each had their hair in two braids either side of their heads. They were all identically matching. The only difference between them was their hair and eye colour, their height, and their age. Their little faces seemed frightened. Their eyes flitted from one girl to the next, as if to try and comfort one another in a distressing time where one could not speak.

They wore cream dresses with frilly lace collars and socks to match. Each had a copy of the Bible in their hands. It was almost military the way they were lined up and coordinated.

A man stood on the stairs. He was quite large and broad. His head was showing the first signs of balding as his jet-black hair had started to recede. He made up for his appearance with his moustache: well groomed and twisted into small points at the ends. He wore a smart, black suit with a pocket watch sitting inside the top pocket of his jacket.

He eyed the girls through dark eyes as he neared the bottom steps. He stopped in front of the first girl, tilting her chin up towards him aggressively. The rest of the girls looked scared, picking at their fingers while the first girl's appearance was inspected.

His knife-like gaze scanned her face and detected a small dirt smudge on her cheek. His head twisted to one side and anger swept across his face as his lips narrowed into a tight line. He brought his arm up high, a black leather-bound copy of the Bible in his hand, as if ready to smack her across the face with its hard surface.

The young girl screwed her face up, her eyes squeezed shut. He had threatened her with his actions, but the book didn't come into contact with her small face. He did it just to scare her. To intimidate her.

"Go and wash your dirty dratted face!" he yelled at her.

The poor girl ran up the stairs as fast as she could, her black, shiny shoes stomping quickly as she flew up each step. The rest of the girls remained as still as stone, as though their master was the Medusa of their home. They looked as though they would crumble at a mere gentle touch. Cracks of fear showed in each of their eyes.

What had he done to these poor girls to make them so afraid? But then she realised. These were Victorian children. In Victorian times it was not unheard of for punishment to include a good whipping, amongst other horrid treatment. Back then you needn't do much to get a beating.

WUH-TSHH!

A loud thrashing sound woke her from her dream. She lay there breathless. Her chest raised up and down quickly. Her heart was like thunder inside her ribcage and sweat trickled down her forehead. There was a thudding deep between her thighs and her nipples had hardened. She couldn't understand why her body had

19

responded in such a way. She was repulsed with herself. Who the hell would get off to children being treated in such a manner? Then she remembered the sound that woke her. *Was it a cane?*

The thought of a firm stick hitting against her skin took her back to a night with her ex. It seemed forever ago. A night when he had treated her to a meal in one of the finest restaurants in town for her birthday. She had been dressed in an emerald green dress that sparkled under the warm lighting. But what really turned the heat up was what she wore underneath: a black, lacy one-piece that barely covered her breasts and left her bare cheeks on show. She had a range of sex toys she had kept in a box under her bed, but that night he had brought something new. A black cane. The sound of the cane snapping in her dream had sparked the same sensations she had felt that night, and all of a sudden she was feeling queasy.

She was disgusted with her reaction. The dream had been of abuse, not a sexy night in with a handsome man between her thighs.

She pushed herself up, putting pressure on her hand, and realised how much it was stinging. Sitting up in her bed, she examined it. Across the back of her hand was a bright red mark, as though someone had smacked it with something. Something thin, something hard. She looked away in disgust as thoughts of the cane hitting her ran through her mind. After taking a breath, she looked back down. The mark was gone.

The nap was meant to make her feel better, but instead she felt worse. The sickness had started to subside, but she felt more confused than ever.

She couldn't help but question whether she had made a rash decision. She knew she had to get away from her fiancé… ex-fiancé, but had this been the wrong move? She decided to give the job a week before making a final decision.

Hanging over the foot of her bed was a light blue, long, flowy skirt and a white blouse. A note was left next to the outfit.

I thought you may like to freshen up for dinner this evening. I believe these may fit you. Lenora.

She lifted the skirt from the bed, and a musty smell arose from it. It smelt old, like it had been stuck for years in a cupboard lingering with dampness. She held the garment up to her waist and looked in the floor-length mirror. She saw it would fit nicely, but it wasn't the only thing she saw in the dusty reflection. A figure stood behind her, causing Jenny to startle.

"Lenora!" Jenny gasped as she swung around. "You startled me." Jenny's heart thudded in her chest, threatening to burst through her ribs.

"Terribly sorry. Do you like the outfit? They don't fit me anymore and were just hanging at the back of my wardrobe. They're all yours if you'd like them, " Lenora offered. She didn't blink once, just stared straight into Jenny's eyes. She made her feel rather on edge. Her heart was still racing slightly as she folded the skirt, laid it on the bed, and picked up the blouse.

"It's lovely, thank you. Perfect for the warm evenings we will have," she replied graciously, hoping she hid her awkwardness well.

"Very good. Well, get changed and be down in the hall in ten minutes. It's salmon and mash tonight." Lenora shut the door behind her and made her way to the hall downstairs.

"Well, that was weird," she whispered to herself. Why did she have a strange feeling about this place already? She had been here only a few hours and already she was getting an iffy vibe from the place *AND* from Lenora. She wondered… had Lenora been snooping around in the room whilst she was sleeping? She hadn't heard the door open, nor seen it open whilst she looked at the clothes. Where had she come from? And she sincerely hoped that Lenora hadn't noticed the look on her face when she smelt the skirt.

"Crap!" She had already lost five minutes thinking about Lenora. She quickly pulled the cotton skirt up over her hips, bringing it to sit on her waist. The smell floated up to her nose and invaded her nostrils. She didn't want to wear the musky thing, but it would be rude not to. She continued to get dressed and pulled on the white blouse, buttoned it up, and tucked it into her skirt. She felt like what she could only describe as an old woman's handbag. Spilt old perfume that almost smelt like cat pee, crushed up mints that had crumbled and stuck to the edges, and an essence of stale Hob Nob biscuits.

She didn't really have time to do anything with her hair, so brushed it back and tied it into a messy bun before slipping her shoes back on and heading out of the room. As she did, she noticed the door had a slight squeak to it as it opened. She hadn't noticed it before. She shook her head, dismissing her thoughts and hurried down the staircase and through to the main hall at the end of the hallway.

The hall was very large and echoed with voices. She was expecting there to be more people here: more children, definitely more teachers, but the hall was half empty. The children were sitting, plates of food laid in front of them as they chatted amongst themselves. Lenora was sitting at the top of the long table on the right of the hall and was waving Jenny over. The room fell silent. Jenny's face was already a little red as she had warmed up from rushing to get dressed and down to the hall, but now her cheeks were flushing for a different reason. She wasn't expecting to have all eyes on her as soon as she entered the room.

"Children, this is Miss Hart. She is the new Art teacher. Let's all make her feel welcome."

A resounding, "Good evening, Miss Hart," echoed around the hall, seemingly bouncing off each wall and back to her.

"Uh, good evening," Jenny replied, looking around at everyone before taking a seat next to Lenora.

The table where she was sitting, she supposed, for the teachers. The children's table was opposite, just as long but on the left-hand side of the hall.

The children resumed their endless chatter, some looking over at her, obviously talking about her and making early judgements. Hopefully nothing too cruel, although one child in particular looked at her with a face of disgust. She knew how children could be, especially when it came to new arrivals. She had been very

22

lucky at her old school. The children were young and always so excited to see her. She didn't expect the same here.

She looked down the long empty table where she had expected the other teachers to be sitting. Where was everyone?

"Lenora, are the other teachers and staff not joining us tonight?" Jenny asked.

"Oh, darling, I forgot to say, the staff don't usually join the children for dinner. They usually stay in their rooms or go out to eat. They're rarely seen in here. It's usually just myself, but now I have you for company." She smiled. Jenny was a little put off by her expression. Her mouth pressed into a forced crescent, almost like she didn't want to smile at all but felt obligated to do so.

Jenny glanced around the hall once more after noticing her dinner plate full of fresh vegetables, salmon, and mashed potatoes. *Where are the kitchen staff or servers?*

Jenny's stomach growled so loudly that Lenora heard it and encouraged her to eat. She really didn't have an appetite this evening, as much as it appeared her stomach had a difference of opinion. Today had been such a blur. One big, confusing blur. Then she remembered her dream.

"You know, when you left my room earlier, I had a nap like you suggested and had the strangest dream."

"Looked like you were having a most pleasant dream to me," Lenora smiled.

"Uh, what do you mean by that?" Jenny asked, feeling a rush of red come over her cheeks. *Was she spying on me while I was sleeping? I knew she must have snuck in to leave those clothes for me, but had she actually been watching me sleep? How much had she seen?* And what Lenora said next would all but confirm her worst nightmare.

"I may look old, my dear, but I'm a woman too. But anyway, let's get back to your strange dream. What was so odd about it?"

Jenny didn't know what to say. It was obvious Lenora had been in the room watching her as she touched herself erotically in her sleep; she had made that quite clear. *Is she some kind of pervert? What the fuck do I even say to that?* Choosing to ignore the

23

situation and avoid humiliating herself further, she focused on the dream she had.

"It was strange. It was like I was a fly on the wall watching a scene before me. A man walking down the stairs; it looked like it was here, the stairs leading to the first floor. The man looked grand, but a nasty essence hung around him. Oh, those poor girls." The hair on her arms stood to attention. She wasn't sure whether it was from the coldness of the room or from retelling her dream.

"Girls?" Lenora questioned. She slid a finger around her neck, freeing it slightly from her tight blouse that had been strangling her. She seemed a little on edge.

"Oh, ignore me. It's just a silly dream." Jenny tried to end the conversation. She had only just met Lenora, and she was starting a new job. She didn't want anyone thinking the new teacher was a psychopath.

"No, go on, dear. I'm all ears. The girls…"

"Yes," Jenny began hastily. "There were girls. They all stood in a line in the hallway at the bottom of the stairs. He was inspecting them. He threatened to hit the first girl because of a small dirt smudge she had missed on her cheek. He was nasty. He had dark hair but was balding and had a scar that went across his eye."

"Hmm, how strange. Follow me." Lenora stood from the table, not having touched a morsel of food from her plate, even though she had been encouraging Jenny to eat. She walked out of the hall and into the dimly lit hallway, leaving the unattended children to finish eating.

There was one girl still staring as Jenny followed Lenora out of the dining hall, her eyes not drifting for a second, not even for her food, which she had not yet touched.

As they stepped into the hallway, she wished she had remembered a cardigan. Her breath was visible in clouds before her as she stood behind Lenora.

Lenora stopped by the stairs and looked around before pulling a set of keys from her pocket. She pushed on one of the planks and it popped open, revealing a small keyhole behind it. She placed one of the many keys into the lock and twisted until it clicked. As

Lenora pulled the key, the panel before them came with it. It was a door.

Lenora flipped a switch and lights lined a stairway leading down to another room. They headed down the steep, wooden steps. They were so rickety they didn't feel safe. Jenny grabbed the handrail to steady herself, but even that was no longer attached to the wall properly. Instead, her hand pressed against the damp, cold wall as they continued down the creaking steps and into the basement below.

Lenora hit another switch at the bottom, and the room filled with light. The space was cluttered with old furniture covered in white sheets, work tools scattered all over the place as if abandoned; it was a complete mess. It looked as though the place was, or had been at some stage, under renovation.

Lenora led her towards the back of the room where there were items stacked on the floor. She pulled a cloth from the top of them, revealing a painting. Dust flew up into the air, causing Jenny to cover her nose and mouth with a cupped hand. The man Jenny had just seen in her dream was there before her, formed from a mixture of paints on a large, flat canvas encased in an old bronze frame.

"But… how?" Jenny whispered.

"So it *is* him?"

"Yes. That's him, tash and all."

"This is Mr Hughes. He once owned this building. Many years ago, this school was an orphanage, homing children of war. Mr Hughes not only owned the property but was also in charge of every member of staff and child. It was a different time back then, and care wasn't like it is today. They were harsher times, and discipline was key to all upbringings."

"Wow, you really know a lot about this place."

"I am the history teacher for a reason, Jenny," she said calmly. "I know a lot about this building, the grounds, and its history. He was very misjudged, in my opinion. He opened the orphanage to help the children and in return just asked for respect, as did most people of that era."

"I believe it was a very harsh time in orphanages back then. I've heard all sorts of horror stories about children being mistreated. Authors over the years have even used the situations as inspiration for stories. Oliver Twist, for example. Everyone knows that one."

"Yes… Oliver," Lenora replied, but her brows were crossed. Did she know of it? *Surely she knows of Oliver, who doesn't? She must have seen it. Surely?* But Lenora's reply didn't sound so sure.

"You know… Please, sir, can I 'ave some more?'" Jenny said, putting on her best cockney accent.

"Uh huh, yep. Anyway, your dream may have just been you picking up on old energy. It can happen with places like this sometimes. Either that or the stress you've been under. You know, the cheating fiancé. Changing schools. It's a lot of change in such a short amount of time."

"I'm sure you're right," Jenny replied, not overly convinced, but what else could it be?

Lenora started to lead Jenny back up the rickety old steps when the lights blew, leaving them in the darkness of the basement.

CHAPTER FOUR
LITTLE SYLVIE

SYLVIE HAD ALWAYS FELT UNWANTED and alone; she was, after all, abandoned on the steps of the orphanage as a baby.

She had been a few days old when the orphanage received her. She was wrapped up in white, knitted blankets and asleep in a wicker basket on that cold, drizzly night.

The other kids at Eden Orphanage made it their job to make sure Sylvie was aware of how unwanted she was. Kids can be cruel.

Sylvie had already had a bad start to the day with Mr Hughes scolding her. That wasn't her fault either. Another girl, Elizabeth, had tricked her.

Every Sunday morning, at six am sharp, all the girls would get up and get themselves ready for church. They had a communal wash space, toilet cubicles on both sides of the room, and wash basins through the middle.

Sylvie had braided her long blonde hair into two plaits that dangled on either side of her head. She did her hair this way every day, and as a result, they were always perfect, not one hair out of place. After checking her hair and being happy with her appearance, she proceeded to wash her face and brush her teeth. She lathered up the soap and scrubbed her freckle-kissed skin hard. Not one speck of dirt or any traces of sweat could be found on her gleaming skin.

Everyone around her was talking to one another whilst getting ready. Some even practised their hymns whilst doing their hair, but no one spoke to Sylvie… They rarely ever did. She didn't like to hang around. She grabbed her toothbrush and flannel and headed back to the dorm room to get dressed.

They wore similar clothing most days, but on Sundays they had matching, cream-coloured, frilly dresses to wear to church, paired with long white socks and black shoes.

She dressed and added a knitted cardigan over the top. There was a chill in the room, probably because the wall had a nice crack in it that Mr Hughes refused to look at. If it wasn't causing a problem for himself, then why bother? At least that was his way of thinking.

A sharp, loud blow of a whistle came from downstairs, and the girls all ran as fast as they could down the polished staircase to where Mr Hughes was waiting for them.

"Sylvie, wait!" Elizabeth said, grabbing her by her arm with one hand. With her other hand, she quickly brushed her hand across her face. "You had something on your cheek."

"Thank you," Sylvie said quietly. Sylvie felt so thankful. The other kids didn't normally talk to her at all, so she was shocked and thankful that Elizabeth had grabbed her quickly before they ran down to Mr Hughes.

"What time do you call this?" He shouted as they all rushed to form a line in the hallway. There was no reply from any of the girls. They were too scared to even look at him, let alone reply. They stood straight in their line, shoulder to shoulder, awaiting their inspections before heading to church.

Sylvie was at the front; not that she wanted to be, but the rest of the girls all pushed her forwards and scrambled past her to make sure they weren't first.

He approached Sylvie, a look of disgust on his face as he tilted her chin to make her look at him. His eyes penetrated her skin, looking for any signs of dirt. Her head, still in his grip, was thrown to one side as he noticed a small dirt smudge on her cheekbone. Anger overcoming him, he drew his arm up high after snatching the copy of the Bible from her quivering hand. He held it high as if ready to smack her across the face with it. Sylvie scrunched her face up, her eyes squeezed shut, preparing herself for the blow across her face. She waited, but nothing hit her.

"Go and wash your dirty, dratted face!" he yelled at her.

She jumped as the voice blasted at her just millimetres away from her face. His breath smelt of sour milk and was irritating her nostrils, but she dared not show it.

The fear flowing through the entirety of her body pushed her to run as fast as she could to the washroom. She sped into the room and rushed to the closest sink where she twisted the cold tap. The water was gushing out of the spout and into her hands. She splashed her face several times and scratched ferociously where Elizabeth had smudged dirt on her cheek.

How could Elizabeth do this? She knew the other girls didn't like her much, but why do this? She didn't even know why they didn't like her to begin with. She hadn't ever done anything to upset or hurt anyone. Salty tears flowed from her bloodshot eyes, trickling down her cheek and mixing with the cold water on her face. Her face cloth was in her room, so her only option was to rub with her bare fingers and nails, causing her face to redden and sting. She took deep breaths as she tried to get herself back together. It would do no good for Mr Hughes to see she had been crying.

"Come on, Sylvie," she whispered to herself. She tried to encourage herself to be strong. No one else would. She was the only person she had to lean on. She took one last deep breath before she headed back down the stairs and reluctantly joined the end of the line, where Mr Hughes would then re-check her appearance. None of the other girls had any problems, just Sylvie.

Elizabeth and the girl next to her smirked as Sylvie re-joined them.

"Something funny, Miss Luanne?" he shot at her.

"N-n-no, sir," she stuttered with fear.

"I didn't think so," he said lowly. He continued to walk over to Sylvie. His eyes looked her up and down before inspecting her face again. He noticed how red it was from scrubbing. "Better." His voice still sounded angry, but at least she didn't get hit... this time.

They headed out the door, one by one as they walked to church. The church was down the road, just past the field. They had to make sure not to dirty their shoes and socks on their way. The church looked run down and forgotten. Weeds were overgrown and nettles spun their way over the fence surrounding the building. At the entrance of the church was a star, right above the doors. The girls all looked up at it as though it was tradition to gaze upon it when entering, but when they did so, the expressions on their faces were of anxiety, not peace.

Sylvie hated church, and upon entering was filled with nerves. The inside of the church was dark. Its walls were painted black and its one beautiful, stained glass window smashed and covered with splintered wooden planks that had been painted. The images were unholy. Scary images that put the girls on edge. A horned beast holding someone by the throat as their lifeless body dripped with blood. A scene portraying hell, its fires embracing people screaming for their lives.

Up ahead was the alter the girls were walking towards in an organised line. It was covered in a black cloth with a silver embroidered symbol. It appeared to be a circle with an upside-down cross inside and surrounded by a pair of twisted antlers. On top of the cloth sat a dagger, a silver goblet, and a black book that held the same symbol upon its cover.

The girls all sat down on the wooden pews, no cushions to add any comfort for them. Sylvie was sat in the front row and kept her eyes focused on her little black shoes, afraid to look up to the man behind the alter.

Mr Hughes stood at the unholy shrine, draped in a black cloak, and the skull what once had been an antelope placed upon his head. His hands were covered in red, the substance dripping from his fingertips. His hands shot up into the air as his voice boomed through the church.

"Praise be to the Dark One." His voice bellowed and the girls all repeated his words in unison.

He placed a bloodied finger over his head and drew an upside-down cross on his forehead. The blood trickled down his head and into the corners of his closed eyes. As he opened them, he revealed eyes of red. Only his dark pupils could be seen amongst the crimson. He looked demonic. An evil entity escaped from the pits of Hell and creating his own following here on earth. Miss Nora worshipped the very ground he walked on, and the girls followed his every word, not out of respect and awe, but out of fear of what he could do to them.

Standing strong and powerful in front of the girls, he read from his evil black book and talked of the Dark Lord and how only he was given permission to use his real name. His demonic name. Only the chosen one was allowed this knowledge. It was to him to pass on the stories and wisdom that the Dark Lord bestowed to him. Each dark teaching was written down in The Dark Lord's Bible.

After a reading from the demonic pages, the girls lined up one by one to receive the right of offering. Tobias, in his dark cloak and scary headdress, took the dagger from the alter. He slowly dragged the sharp blade across his plump, scarred palm. Blood oozed from his flesh, dripping onto the cold, stone ground. He raised his hand over the top of the first girl's head.

"With this blood, the Dark Lord grants you a space with him in the afterlife. His loyal subjects shall be rewarded forever more."

The girl tipped her head back and opened her mouth. Her eyes squeezed tightly shut. She didn't want this, but she had no other choice. A drop of blood dripped from Tobias's firm fist and onto her tongue. The taste of iron flooded her mouth and made her feel sick.

Each of the girls, including Miss May, had to go through with the rights before leaving the church.

After church, the children had chores to do around the home. Each of them had a weekly chore chart pinned to the wall in the hallway. The pieces of paper were attached to a square sheet of cork. The Assistant Head hated to remind the children of their chores all the time, so she came up with the system. Mr Hughes believed it to be ingenious.

His assistant was always brown-nosing. Always wanting his approval. She sat him upon a pedestal like a god and worshipped the ground he walked on. He could do no wrong in her eyes. So, when he agreed to the chore charts, she was over the moon. The chores she had set for the girls included washing the floors by hand, polishing the staircase and paintings, chimney sweeping, cleaning the windows, making the beds, and cleaning the kitchen.

As soon as they came in through the door, Sylvie headed straight to the notice board where their chore lists were pinned. Each of them had a piece of paper attached to the board with their name at the top, a list of chores, and the days they were to do them.

Today, Sylvie and another child were scheduled to clean the floors. She rushed up the stairs to her room to get changed. No way could they ever do any chores, or anything else for that matter, in their Sunday best. These clothes were for church only. If they were to get a spot of dirt on them, even from the church, they would be in trouble. Mr Hughes made it very evident it would not just be himself they would displease, but their Lord as well. He was almighty and would bestow punishment on all who disobeyed and didn't have pride in their appearance.

She changed into a brown, long-sleeved dress and placed a stained apron over the top. It had one pocket in the front to carry cleaning products and still had a rag in it from her last lot of chores. She went to the supply cupboard and grabbed a bucket to fill with water and soda, as well as a broom so she could sweep thoroughly before washing the floors.

As she carried the bucket and broom down the stairs, there was one girl already making a start on polishing the stair banister: the girl who had been standing with Elizabeth when they had been looked over in their Sunday clothes that morning. Carrying the broom and bucket was awkward when you were trying to make your way down the stairs. To make things worse, the girl noticed Sylvie was struggling, but instead of helping her, she stuck her foot out just as Sylvie was taking her next step. Sylvie went crashing down the stairs, the broom and bucket making a racket as they bounced and crashed down each step before joining her at the bottom, the broom hitting her hard on the head.

The girl who had tripped her stifled her laugh as she heard footsteps coming their way and quickly got back to polishing the banister. The Assistant Head came stomping into the hallway demanding to know what was going on.

"What the hell do you think you're playing at?" she whispered angrily at Sylvie. She didn't even help her up or make sure Sylvie was okay. Instead, she continued to scold her. "Any more noise from you and Mr Hughes will not be a very happy man. You're already in trouble after this morning's mischief. This is your final warning, Sylvie!"

"But, miss…"

"No, *but miss,* anything! End of, Sylvie. Get on with your chores… in silence!"

She wasn't even able to tell her what had actually happened. She had done nothing wrong and was still in the bad books. It shouldn't be her being told off, it should be that Elizabeth and her idiot of a friend. They deserved the bad treatment Sylvie was getting. Sylvie didn't have anyone in this place: no friends, no family, she couldn't even depend on her caregivers, if you could even call them that.

She picked up the metal bucket and wooden broom, and as she did, they clanged together. Her eyes shut tight as soon as the noise rattled through the hall, but no sign of the Assistant Head.

"You were lucky that time," the girl on the stairs smirked at her.

Sylvie didn't reply, she just carried on with her chores, ignoring the girl's sneering remarks. She made her way out into the garden and fetched water from the well. This was the only water the girls were allowed to use. Mr Hughes had water plumbed to his en-suite, but everyone else had to use the well water, and at that time of year, it was freezing. She attached the bucket to the damp rope hanging on the side of the well and sent the bucket plummeting down into the icy cold water.

The bucket, now full, was heavy, and she had to be careful not to spill any as she entered the hallway. She placed the bucket to one side and swept throughout the hallway before making a start on washing the floors. Once the floors had been swept of any dust, she propped the broom against the wall and added bicarbonate of soda to the water in the bucket. She grabbed her floor brush with its tough bristles and dunked it into the mixture. She hated the mixture and what it did to her hands. It always left her skin feeling rough and bumpy, like an old man's hands. Not the hands of a child at all. Her hands should be clean and soft, with neatly filed nails. Instead, they resembled the hands of someone who had already worked their whole life, callused and chapped, and her nails were almost non-existent. Broken and chipped away from all the chores she did on a daily basis. Not to mention, due to nerves, she would bite any nails remaining down so much that they would bleed.

Sylvie cleaned from the front door all the way through to the kitchen door. Her hands were sore and her knees throbbing from where she had been scrubbing so hard on the tiled floor. The kitchen door opened as Sylvie was washing the skirting board next to it. The girl leaving the kitchen screamed out of shock and dropped the china bowl and jug. Pieces of smashed china flew across the wet, shiny floor and a door upstairs slammed.

"Now you've done it." The girl cleaning the stairs had moved to the windows and stood there shaking her head at Sylvie.

"It wasn't me, was it? I'm cleaning the skirting board, it's not like I tripped her."

"We'll see whom Mr Hughes believes, shall we?" the girl from the kitchen said smugly.

"But I didn't do anything!" She was really panicking. After what had happened that morning, Miss-Knickers-in-a-Twist told her off for her fall down the stairs, and now this!

"What on earth do you girls think you're playing at? I am trying to work, and you've disturbed me for the last time!" he shouted at the three of them.

"It was her, sir," she pointed at Sylvie. "It was Sylvie. She tripped Rose as she was bringing the bowl and jug back out, sir." Her voice sounded so innocent and angelic.

"Oh, did she now? That's it for you, Sylvie. You tidy up this mess. Right now!"

Sylvie ran to the closet, sliding across the wet floor as she did, to grab a pan and brushed the china up as quickly as she could. He watched her every movement.

"Quick!" he bellowed. She rushed to the kitchen and threw the sharp shards into the bin.

"Now, you'll come with me." Pure aggression filled his voice.

"Please, sir, no." She cried, knowing exactly what was coming next. "Please, sir, it wasn't my fault."

"Of course, it wasn't. Rose just happened to scream and drop everything for no reason, huh?" Sarcasm dripped from each word.

"I don't know why she screamed. PLEASE!!" she begged through her tears.

He dragged her up the stairs and through his office door and took the cane from the wall next to his desk. He pushed her against the table where he had previously been working and pulled her dress up, revealing the upper parts of her legs.

WUH-TSHH!

Sylvie screamed as the cane snapped against her pale legs, a hot, red line starting to form. Before the mark fully formed to a welt, he went again.

WUH-TSHH!

She screamed again. So much pain. The sting from the cane felt as though her skin was on fire. Lines burned onto her skin, her heart racing so fast she thought she would pass out from the pain. He pulled her dress back down covering the scald marks he had left her with.

"And for one final measure to make sure this sinks in," he started. He dragged her out of his office and back downstairs towards the back door. "You shall spend the next hour outside thinking about what you have done today and how you will improve your behaviour in the future."

Sylvie was crying in pain, dangling behind him as he pulled her by her wrist through the doors and threw her hard to the snow-covered ground.

She didn't even have her cardigan, just her dress and apron. She was beside herself with grief and shivering with cold. The stinging from the cuts left by the cane was at least being cooled by the icy snow she was now sitting in.

CHAPTER FIVE
THE BULLY

"**GOOD MORNING, EVERYONE,**" Jenny greeted her students as she stood from her seat at the front of the classroom.

"Good morning, Miss Hart," they said in unison.

"Miss Tart." One of the girls in the back sniggered. The same girl who had been staring at her the night before in the dining hall.

"Excuse me? What is your name?" Jenny asked patiently.

"Lizzie, Miss," she replied with a smirk.

"And what did you mean by that statement, Lizzie?"

"Just that we all know you and Miss May seem to have had a little alone time in the basement last night... with the lights off too." A few of the girls sitting around Lizzie giggled.

"Well, I can assure you all that you have heard wrong. Miss May was showing me around and as we were coming back up the stairs a bulb blew causing the fuse to go as well. Not that I have to explain myself to a group of children. You are all here to learn, not to gossip. So on that note, let's begin." She turned on the spot and headed back to her desk.

"Today we will be learning about Salvador Dali," she began.

"Has anyone heard of him?" A girl towards the middle of the class slowly raised her hand. "Yes, what's your name?"

"Abigail, Miss. Salvador Dali was a Spanish artist, Miss. He was known for his works portraying horror and trauma. Many of his pieces included skulls and faces, some even appearing to be melting."

"Well, Abigail, I am certainly impressed with your knowledge. Seems you will do well on this subject." She smiled. "As the electrics have been a bit of an issue, we have to make do with what we have to hand." She proceeded to stick up an A3 painting she had done first thing this morning.

She hadn't slept well and when she had awoken at four-thirty, she decided to get to work. She had gone to the art room and painted Salvador Dali's *The Face Of War*. She had the painting spot on. One large, skeletal face looked worried, its brow stressing the amount of fear it was holding onto. In place of its eyes and open mouth were more faces, and inside those faces, more faces! It was creepy and not an image you could un-imagine quickly. Snake-like creatures seemed to slither into attack around the main head. The painting was full of terror.

As Jenny attached the painting to the whiteboard, the girls started whispering; some were shocked by the image before them.

"This is a copy of Salvador Dali's painting *The Face Of War*. Who would like to tell me what it makes them feel or what thoughts come to you when looking at this painting?" Jenny glanced around. No hands were raised. Were they making this class hard on purpose? She started to walk around the desks as she decided whom to call upon. A girl sat next to Lizzie exchanging stupid faces with Lizzie, clearly not interested in the class at all.

"Louise, is it?" The girl rolled her eyes and looked up at her.

"Uh, yeah," she said, giving Jenny some attitude.

"Well, Louise, look at the painting. What does it make you feel? Is there anything you want to say about it?" She walked back to her desk at the front of the class.

"It's weird and the artist was probably high when he painted it."

"Oh, come on, Louise. You must have more than that. How does it make you feel?"

"I don't know… uncomfortable?"

"And why does it make you feel that?"

"Hello?? It's got heads within heads within heads!"

"And does anyone know why Dali painted the heads within each other in such a way?" Jenny asked. One small hand raised and Jenny smiled.

"Yes, Abigail?"

"I believe he painted faces within faces to represent the feeling of being uncomfortable with the continuing of wars and the horror of the war and trauma it was creating throughout the world."

"Wow, Abigail, you really know your art! Exactly. This painting was created to project the emotions felt around the Spanish civil war, the horror and fear of death, and future wars.

"The faces within faces symbolise an infinite fear of war continuing over and over. At the time of this painting, you will find that the Spanish civil war had just finished and World War II was ongoing, so it was very fitting for the time he painted this.

"So, for today's task, I would like you to come up with your own painting depicting things that may be going on in the world today."

The girls all headed in different directions to get the equipment they needed. Some already had sketchbooks out, others went to get big A3 pieces of paper from the cupboard, and others were choosing between gouache, acrylic, or watercolour paints to use.

Jenny walked around the class seeing how everyone was doing. Some obviously had more talent than others, but at least they were trying. She noticed a couple of paintings based on poverty, children drawn in scraggy clothes and begging for money on streets, and tidal waves full of trash. She noticed Abigail's piece. Instead of paints, she had used charcoals on a white A3 sheet of paper. Large, black smudges around the edge of the material drew the eyes inwards to the centre of the scene: the face of a young girl, her fingers digging into her fleshy skin. Her eyes were black and hollow, and her mouth was drawn into a scream. She looked in pain yet empty. As if all emotion had drained from her.

"Abigail, what a haunting image. You have definitely nailed the brief. Can you tell me your inspiration and meaning behind this piece?" Jenny asked as she admired her work.

"Haha! Look, it's Abigail's self-portrait whilst straining a-" Lizzie began, but Jenny shut her down before she could finish.

"Lizzie, enough! Go to Miss May this instant!" Jenny demanded.

"Ugh, fine. Your class is a boring pile of-"

"LIZZIE, NOW!" Jenny shouted across the room to where Lizzie was still sitting and rolling her eyes. Lizzie finally left the room, but not before shooting Jenny a horrid smirk and closing the door behind her.

"Sorry, Abigail, Your art is beautifully done. She probably acted out of jealousy; most bullies do."

The class turned to look at the paper left on Lizzie's desk and giggled. It seemed that all Lizzie could muster up was a stick man holding what looked to be another stick. No imagination or effort had been shown at all.

Jenny couldn't stop thinking about Abigail's work. How dark and empty it was, yet it had a hint of desperation, a child that was scared, but of what? The children shouldn't have anything to be afraid of here. It was a school and basically their home. Their parents had paid very well for the girls to have their education here. A place where they could also live and be looked after while their parents were working and away overseas. What had been Abigail's inspiration?

CHAPTER
SIX
SNOWY GRAVE

SYLVIE WAS SHIVERING, her knees held tightly against her chest as she sat in the wet snow. The winter sun had started to withdraw and the sky began to darken. Tears fell from her eyes and stung her grazed knees as she cried. They froze almost instantly as they dropped onto her bare skin.

Her knees were already scratched up and bruised from crawling around cleaning the floors, and now they were being covered by icy tears. Her fingertips were so cold they had started to stiffen. She tried to warm them by cupping her hands to her face and blowing warm breath into them, but as she did she noticed her fingers were unable to move. They remained rigid, as though her hands were made from clay and stuck in a bowled position.

Scared she may freeze to death, she pushed herself up slowly up from the frostbitten ground and fell against the icy door. She reached to twist the handle, but as she tried to move her fingers and touch the metal handle, shocks went through the remaining nerves that were able to feel anything and sent burning pains into her hands.

She couldn't use her hands, so she tried her voice instead.

41

"Please?" Her voice was raspy and quiet as she tried to call through the door. "Please? Please let me in?" she begged. She couldn't hear anyone, so she frigidly made her way to look through the windows of the hall. Everyone should be having dinner now.

She trod slowly through the ever-deepening snow, leaving a long trail behind her. The snow reached up to her knees, so the trail behind her was made up of long, deep lines rather than footsteps. She made it around to the windows of the hall and could see everyone sitting down at the tables, eating something hot. She couldn't make out what it was as the glass had fogged up slightly on the inside, blurring the scene before her.

She tried to bang on the window, but the act sent pains through her wrist. The knock was so faint due to her weakness and pain that no one heard the tap on the window. She held her arms on the windowpanes, leant her head against them, and continued to call out.

"Anyone? P-p-p-please! I'm c-c-cold," her teeth chattered.

But still, no one heard her cries for help. Exhaustion was becoming the better of her as her energy started to fail. Her eyes closed slowly and she fell into the snow. She lay on the ground, a snowy wall encasing her. Her soft skin grew paler and almost matched the snow she lay in. The trees around the grounds were swaying in the wintry wind, and the snowflakes continued to fall and settle upon any untouched surfaces, including little Sylvie. Her eyelashes lay still and white, snowflakes delicately decorating them, and her once petal pink were lips coated in ice, giving them a blue glossy effect.

Everyone finished their meals and it was time for the kitchen staff to clean up and the children to do their evening reading. The girls headed to the library to pick their books for the night. This was the only time they were allowed to enter the library. It was large and dark with only a few candles laid out for light. The bookcases were so large they required a ladder to reach the higher shelves. The higher shelves were Mr. Hughes' own collection of books and articles and were not to be touched by anyone, not even the other members of staff. His books looked old. Many of them had weird symbols down their spines.

The girls chose which books they would read and headed up to the dormitory to read before washing and going to bed.

The kitchen staff were left to clean the hall and kitchen. After running out of water to wash the tables, they headed outside to the well to fetch more water. Nancy placed a knitted shawl around her shoulders and grabbed the bucket from one of the hall tables that had just been cleaned. They always started with the tables rather than the floors, so that any remaining crumbs from the tables would fall to the floor when they wiped them down and could then be cleaned up.

She made her way to the door leading outside to the gardens. She opened the door, and the icy wind blew the fresh, powdery snow inside. She placed the key into her apron pocket and walked over to the well, hoping it hadn't iced over yet.

The snow was deep ,and the wind was howling, making it hard for Nancy to see where she was going. Her foot collided with something big and hard, and she fell into the deep snow. As she turned and opened her eyes, she was shocked to see a head beside her. She screamed as loudly as she could, but no one heard her screams. She left the bucket in the snow and ran, as much as she was able to, through the snow and back indoors.

Her hands were shaking so much, not just from the cold, but from seeing Sylvie's little body stiff in the snow. She took the key from her pocket and fumbled with it to open the door. As soon as she heard the lock click, she sprinted clumsily through the entrance screaming for help, leaving wet footprints all over the floor.

"Help! A little girl is dead out there!" she screamed as she ran down the hallway and into the library. "Sir, Sir!"

Mr Hughes was in the library, part way up a ladder reaching for a black book from one of the higher shelves, when Nancy threw herself into the room.

"A girl… dead… in the snow," she said between breaths as her chest rushed up and down.

43

"What girl? They should all be in their rooms reading. You must be mistaken." But then he remembered. He had completely forgotten he had left Sylvie outside as her punishment earlier in the day. "Don't worry, Nancy, I will look into this. Leave it to me," he comforted her. "Please, head home for the day," he finished. He acted so calmly, when, in fact, inside he was panicking.

"Yes, Sir. Thank you, Sir," she replied and headed back to the kitchen to get her things.

"Damn it!" he growled as he punched the table. The brandy in his glass jumped over the edge as the pummel vibrated through it. He grabbed his drink and downed it in one swallow before starting to pace the room. What was he to do? He couldn't alert the authorities, there would be too many questions, he wouldn't want anyone to know the mistake he had made. And he couldn't tell his Lord. He wouldn't want him to know he had neglected a child and left her to die out in the cold. *But what if he already knows? What if she is there with him on the other side?*

He ran his hand through his hair as his heart raced with anxiety. He didn't really worry about the young girl. To be honest, he couldn't care less whether she was dead or alive. One less kid to look after. One less mouth to feed. He was more worried about himself. What would happen to him if anyone found out?

He grabbed the bottle of brandy, and instead of pouring himself another glass, he took a large swig straight from the bottle and leant on his desk as he tried to work out what to do with the body.

His assistant was walking past the library and heard his footsteps as he paced the room. She opened the door slightly to find he had stopped walking the lengths of the library and was leant against the desk, a look of distress across his face, his head bowed down.

"Toby?" she called as she stepped quietly inside and closed the door. "Is everything okay?"

"No. No, it's not," he sighed.

"Is it something I can help with? You know you can talk to me about anything." And she really did mean it. She would do anything for this man; he had no idea how much she worshipped him.

"I don't know."

She moved next to him and placed her hand on top of his.

"You can trust me." She smiled lustily at him as his gaze met hers.

"Nora, this is a very arduous situation, and I'm not sure it is for a lady to deal with."

"Well, let me be the judge of that." She took his hands in hers, making him turn towards her. He let out a frustrated sigh.

"Okay, but you mustn't tell a soul. If anyone finds out about this, I'm a dead man."

"You can trust me, Toby." She started to worry about what it might be. What was causing him to panic so?

"It's that girl, Sylvie."

"Oh, what has she gone and done now? I've had just about enough of that little brat today."

"She's dead. I put her outside for an hour as part of her punishment, to make her think about how she has been acting."

"And so you should have!"

"But it wasn't just an hour. I forgot about her, and the door was locked so she couldn't come back in until I let her. She froze to death."

"Oh, Toby. It's not your fault. You're a very busy man, and if she hadn't been messing around then she wouldn't have had to be punished, would she? Discipline is important; you were only doing your job."

"Oh, if only everyone would see it that way, but I'm almost sure they wouldn't, Nora. I don't know what to do with her body."

"Does anyone else know about this?" she questioned thoughtfully.

"Just the woman who found her, one of the kitchen staff. Oh, what's her damn name… Nancy!"

"Oh, you want to be careful with that one. She can spread rumours quickly. Where is she?"

"I sent her home."

"Good. At least she can't spread rumours around the kitchen staff. She will need sacking, though."

"You say she would spread rumours? I think she will need more than sacking. What's to stop her from spreading rumours to the community? We can't have them turning up here, or the church for that matter. Especially the church." He knew he had to do something more about Nancy. If only he had found the body himself; better yet, better if he hadn't forgotten about Sylvie at all.

"I could take care of her. I know it doesn't particularly put me in a good light, but I want to help you. You shouldn't be punished for this. That girl Nancy can be a sly one. I wouldn't have any trouble seeing to her not being around anymore. We could pop round to see her and have a chat about what she had seen. I will offer her a cake made with carbolic acid, and she will be none the wiser."

"You're going to poison her with cleaning powder?" He thought about what she suggested. What he had just done was manslaughter; were they now about to add murder to the list too?

"Sure, many people mistake it for baking powder anyway, so when she is found dead at her own home, they'll think she accidentally poisoned herself. I'll head to her home with some cakes. It will look as though she had been baking."

"Nora, you are wicked, but you are a genius."

His body filled with testosterone as he planned with Nora. He whisked her off the floor and placed her on the table beside him. Her legs were spread on either side of his body as he stood facing her. His heartbeat was racing. He ran his hand into her hair, wrapped it around his hand, and pulled it back. He started to kiss her neck, gently, then as if nothing ever happened, he walked away from her and out the door.

What on earth was that all about? she thought. She was left sitting on the table, wanting more. Her legs quivering, her breath fast. Why had he stopped and walked away? Was he playing with her? He had her wrapped around his little finger. She was completely mesmerised by him, as if under a spell.

She climbed down from the table, smoothed out her clothes, and left the library to see where he had gone. Closing the door behind her, she could hear his footsteps heading towards the back door.

She followed him out into the snow. The white flakes had stopped falling from the sky, but what had fallen was now so deep she wondered how a child could even attempt to walk through it. The snow seeped through her shoes, leaving her feet and legs cold and wet. The wind was glacial, bitter, as it hit her skin. She forced herself against the whipping cool air to walk over to Toby Hughes. Lying in the white drift was the small body of little Sylvie.

"What shall we do with her, Toby?"

He looked up at her and then towards the woods.

"This is something I need to do, Nora. Why don't you send all the staff home and get started on those cakes?"

"Are you sure? I don't mind helping you out here first," she continued, willing to do anything for him.

"Thank you, Nora, but yes, I'm sure. I don't want you to get ill from the cold. Go in and get warm in the kitchen. This shouldn't take too long," he said as he eyed up the shed.

Nora made her way back inside whilst Toby tramped through the thick snow over to the wooden hut.

He struggled with the door against the weight of the snowdrift, but managed to drag it open just enough to squeeze inside. He would need something to dig with and a way to help to move the body. The shed was full of gardening tools, flowerpots, and a bench for potting. They used it for planting their fruits and vegetables during the spring and summer months. He looked around for something he could use.

In the dark, it was hard to make out what was in front of him. His hands fumbled around the wall to guide him, but in doing so he knocked a box of nails from the shelf. He heard them scatter all over the wooden floorboards. He continued clumsily to the back of the shed where he felt a long wooden handle. The spade. And to the left of it was a wheelbarrow. It would be hard to manoeuvre, but what other choice did he have? He couldn't just drag her body.

Dead bodies were heavy, and this one's clothes were drenched from soaking up the snow surrounding her. She would be very awkward to move, and now that the storm had stopped, she had started to ice over. He grabbed the wheelbarrow, turned it upright onto its wheel, and chucked the spade inside before starting to wheel it out.

"FUUUCCKKK!!" Toby screamed out in pain. He had forgotten about the nails he had knocked over. His foot slipped over one, causing him to lose his balance and place his foot through a rusty nail that was pointing out of a piece of old fence he had been meaning to get rid of. The plank was now attached to his foot, the nail having shot right through the sole of his shoe and into his flesh.

As he screamed out, he dropped the wheelbarrow and started pounding the workbench with his fist. Nora was inside so couldn't hear his profanity. He leant against the wooden wall and pulled his foot up, resting it on his other leg. His fingers felt along the splintered wood that was one with him. He tugged it a little and felt a throb in his foot. Taking a deep breath and squeezing his eyes shut, he grasped the plank tightly in his hands and pulled as quickly as he could. The nail dragged against and out of his flesh, blood dripping into the darkness as it oozed out through his sole.

With it free from him, he threw the rough piece of wood as hard as he could in anger without thinking. He huffed and growled swear words under his breath, picked up the wheelbarrow and spade, and dragged his feet along the floor so he wouldn't slip on another nail. Instead, he heard them rolling around his feet as he shuffled towards the shed door. Putting pressure on his injured foot made it beat with its own pulse. Pain thumped every time he leant on it.

He smashed the wheelbarrow against the entrance in an attempt to force the door open. But the snow against it was so dense it barely budged. He thought about ramming the door again, but instead grabbed the spade and squeezed back into the snow. Spade in hand, half tempted to throw it in anger but resisting, he dug a trench in the snow behind the back of the door so it could fully open. It swung open and he threw the spade back into the wheelbarrow, making enough noise to wake the dead.

The next challenge was getting back to Sylvie through the snow. He pushed the wheelbarrow out of the doorway and against the resistance.

Once he made it back, he had completely forgotten the pain in his foot, probably due to the numbing effect of the snow. He took the spade out and replaced it with Sylvie's heavy, frozen body. Her body sounded as though it was snapping as the ice building up on her skin cracked. He didn't even look at her. Just picked her up and shoved her in the wheelbarrow and laid the spade next to her, showing more kindness to a tool rather than the young girl who he had left to die.

He started to make his way to the woodland at the edge of the garden, the snow compacting below his shoes and making crunching noises with every step, until he reached a small clearing just big enough to bury her small body. Digging the earth was more difficult than he had originally imagined. He believed the snow would have made the ground wet enough for the spade to glide through the dirt. What he had failed to remember was that the trees were so dense that the ground had just a sprinkle of snow, almost like a frozen cake sprinkled with icing sugar.

Failing to dig very deep, he had a small hole dug out very close to the surface that was just barely big enough for Sylvie's small body. He threw her into her final resting place: a reflection of her life, alone and away from anyone that had any ability of love and kindness. He shovelled the freshly dug dirt back on top of her tiny body until the hole was completely filled. To make sure no one would ever stumble upon her, he dragged a rock over her resting place and made sure to add a few fallen branches and twigs to make it look more natural.

As he made his way out of the woods, snowflakes were once again falling and had started to fill the hole where Sylvie once lain.

CHAPTER SEVEN
THE STORM BEGINS

LIGHTNING ENCASED THE CLASSROOM like a blanket surrounding the building. The girls sitting at their desks, all screamed as a loud clap of thunder shook the room. The rain started falling in sheets, only visible when the lightning struck, but the sound of the rain hitting the windows was deafening. Jenny was having to shout for her voice to be heard above the impact of the water thrashing against the glass.

"Girls, please settle down! I'm sure the storm will pass soon!"

Lenora entered the classroom, holding a candle to light the way. The whole building was now in darkness, just as they were about to finish their first lesson.

"Children!" Lenora shouted. "Please go to the library, choose your books, and head to your rooms to read. Classes are cancelled for the remainder of the day!" she announced.

"Yes, Miss!" they could just about hear the girls say in unison as they packed up their supplies and headed out of the art room.

"Jenny, I have sent the other teachers home, as they live farther afield and I didn't want them getting stuck here away from their families. It will just be you and me holding the fort I'm afraid."

"Oh, okay, not to worry. I'm sure the girls have things they can do in their rooms for now. I can always give them extra bits to do."

"Thank you, Jenny. I don't know what you want to do with the rest of your day now. Usually, when the other teachers aren't on duty, they take the chance to go into town or tie up any unfinished marking or lesson plan."

"Well, I had been wanting to check out the library. I do love books."

"Oh, please do! Have you read *Romeo and Juliet*? I would definitely recommend it."

"To be honest, I'm more of a horror fan myself. I'm a massive Stephen King fan."

"Oh, well, you may not find any of those in there."

"That's okay, I'm sure I'll find something," she smiled politely.

"By all means," Lenora smiled back and walked out of the room.

"Okay, that was weird," Jenny whispered to herself. She couldn't shake the weird feeling she got from Lenora, especially when she acted so normal. She shook her head, picked up her painting and planner, and headed out of the room and upstairs towards the library.

She held the planner and painting under her arm as she made her way up the stairs, her hand gliding up the banister feeling the deep contours of the wood under palm. The school was quiet apart from the sound of rain and thunder. It was perfect for reading, so peaceful. Jenny loved the sound of pitter-patter whilst she read. Now to find the perfect book to accompany the weather.

As she stepped into the library, candles were already lit around the room. The windows looked out onto the front drive. Or what *was* the front drive. It was starting to look more like a pond. The amount of rain that had fallen in the last twenty minutes had collected in the drive and had started to flood. The other teachers were lucky to have left when they did. She paced towards the bookcase after picking up a candle from the small table by the door. Lifting the candle, she looked through the shelves of books. There were many classics such as Shakespeare's *A Midsummer Night's Dream*, F. Scott Fitzgerald's *The Great Gatsby*, John Steinbeck's *Of Mice and Men*, and many more. She wasn't really into the classics. She had read *Of Mice and Men* when she was studying for her English exam at school. Although she enjoyed it, it was not something she wanted to read again. A bit too on the sad side for her liking. She could deal with horror and thrillers, but *Of Mice and Men* was neither of those.

Her hand swept along the long row of books as her eyes skimmed the titles. She came to one book with no title. It was small and rough around the edges. The black cover faded to a dark grey with the initial 'S' in the bottom right corner. She pulled the book forward and off the shelf. Flipping the front of the book open, the first page was blank with a small message at the top.

Property of Sylvie
Hands off!

"Who are you?" Jenny whispered. She decided she was going to find out exactly who Sylvie was. She couldn't remember a Sylvie in her class. Her classroom held all the students attending the school, so she didn't feel too afraid of overstepping and invading anyone's privacy. She headed out of the library and to her bedroom, book in hand.

She lit the two candles that sat by her bed and left the curtain open so she could see the storm in her peripheral vision. There was a slight chill in her room, unusual for this time of year, so she balanced a few logs ontop of eachother and started a fire. The rain tapped against her window, and the flickering light of the candles and flames inside the fireplace made the room feel cosy. She curled up on her bed, pulled a small blanket over her knees, and opened the diary to the first page.

12th October 1876

Dear Diary,
Today has been hard. I know the other girls don't really like
me and most of the time I'm okay with that and do my own thing.
Today though has been different. I felt so lonely. I was reading a
book I got from the library and one of the girls started laughing
at me. The other girls are ahead of me in their reading skills and
are reading the bigger books. I'm still on the small kids' books. I
wish I could be better at reading.
I did ask Miss Nora for help but she was busy helping
Elizabeth. I listened to her reading out loud. It was called
Twenty Thousand Leagues Under the Sea. From what I heard,
some people thought their boat was being attacked by a nasty
monster. They went looking for it and instead of finding a
monster, they found a man called Captain Nemo in a submarine!
I wonder what it's like in the sea. It sounds scary. I think it's
scary here though so it wouldn't make a difference to me. At least
Mr. Hughes couldn't whip me anymore.
I don't like his whip. It really hurts. The last time he punished
me, he used a wooden ruler on my knuckles. He thinks I should be
writing better by now, using bigger words. But I struggle with the
big words. I don't know how to get better. Miss Nora doesn't
have time for me, and the other girls won't help me.
If I could escape onto a submarine, I could get far, far away.
Maybe find a new family. I might find people in the sea just like
the people from Elizabeth's book did. And maybe those people
would like me and help me. Maybe one day someone will find me
and like me. I wish that day would be soon. I don't like being
alone. Everyone else plays games together, but they won't let me
play with them. I try but always get told to go away. They don't
know how far away I want to go.
I wish so much I could.
Hopefully, tomorrow is better.
Goodnight,
Sylvie.

"Oh, you poor thing." Jenny held back tears.

There was nothing she could do for her. She looked back at the date of the first entry. 12th October 1876. Definitely not one of her students. She would never let any of her students feel this way. How could anyone let a child feel so alone?

Jenny continued hastily onto the next page.

19th October 1876

Dear Diary,

I've not been able to write. Mr. Hughes hit my hands again. He said I didn't clean the windows properly and when I gave him his dinner it was cold. I tried to tell him it was the kitchen's fault and I only brought the food to him, but he didn't believe me. No one ever believes me.

So I had ten lashings of the ruler on my fingers. They hurt so much, but Miss Nora made me write still and it hurt so bad. It felt like my heartbeat was in my fingers.

I had to wrap my fingers up so I could do the chores too. Why are they like this? I haven't done anything wrong.

Away from here, I want to be,
Away from the pain and be happy.
Far away in the warm sunshine,
with a family I can call all mine.

They will take me on trips,
Not threaten me with whips.
They will cuddle me.
They will love me.

I will love them too,
For everything they do.

I wish, oh I wish,
I had a family to go to.

I'm calling this poem 'I Wish.' Maybe one day I can put it in a
newspaper or a book for people to read. Maybe I will keep
writing poems and hope it helps me get better and use bigger
words like Mr. Hughes wants me to.

Goodnight,
Sylvie

Jenny jumped as a loud crash of thunder rumbled through her room, shaking everything around her, including the bed she was curled up on. The book flew out of her hands, knocking the candle over from the bedside table onto the rug. She leapt off the bed and grabbed the candle, but the flame had already started to burn the rug. She stomped on the small flames to put them out before they spread any further, but in doing so, she had unintentionally informed Lenora that there was a problem due to all the noise she was making.

Lenora went running into the room, candle in hand.

"What is it? What's wrong? Are you okay?" she asked in a panic.

"Yes. Sorry. I guess the storm made me jump whilst I was reading, and I knocked the candle over. I am so sorry. I will pay to replace it."

Lenora had a look of annoyance spread across her face, but as she faced Jenny, she continued on as if she didn't mind at all.

"Oh, don't worry about that old thing. It probably needed replacing anyway." She turned away before Jenny could reply and headed out of the door.

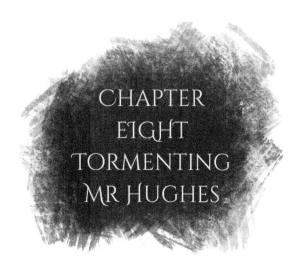

CHAPTER EIGHT
TORMENTING MR HUGHES

SNOW FELL ONTO MR. HUGHES SHOULDERS as he walked past the hole in the snow where Sylvie had once lain and continued back inside. The warmth was inviting, and the smell of cakes lingered in the air through the hall from the kitchen. Nora had been busy preparing cakes for the kitchen girl. Not ordinary cakes. Cakes to poison Nancy who had found Sylvie's body stiff in the snow. Although they smelt truly tempting, Mr. Hughes had to remember not to taste a crumb of what Nora was rustling up.

"These smell divine," he said as he admired the smell and the sight of them. "They look truly delicious." He picked up one of the buns. So light, and as he squeezed it, he could tell just how fluffy they must be on the inside. Nora had decorated the buns with lavender-flavoured icing. The scent of the lavender mixed with the sweet smell of cake and icing, creating a mouth-watering treat.

"You mustn't try them, Toby," she warned as she iced the last bun. "You'd regret it if you did. They would taste nice, but you'd end up dead."

"Can't be having that now, can we?" He smiled at her menacingly.

"Not at all," she smiled back at him, full of lust. "In the morning, I shall visit her myself. I'll go early enough that her neighbours won't see me. No one will ever know I've been there."

"Thank you, Nora. I shall not forget this," he replied. "Now, I must get to bed, as should you. It will be a long day tomorrow, especially since you'll be leaving early in the morning."

"Yes, you head off. I'll tidy up here and take myself off to bed shortly."

"Thank you again, Nora," he said as he headed back into the hall, shutting the kitchen door behind him. He made his way along the hallway towards the stairs when the back door flew open.

BANG! The door sounded as it hit the wall. The wind had thrown the door wide open, sending a freezing gust inside, along with a flurry of snow. He ran over to shut it, goosebumps appearing all over his skin under his white shirt, as the cold air blew around him.

"Damn this door!" he said angrily to himself as he shut it. This time he made sure he locked it. He turned his key in the lock and jiggled the handle aggressively to make sure it stayed shut. He huffed and continued making his way to the staircase. At the bottom of the stairs, he grabbed the candle placed on the small table by the front door.

The candle flame flickered and almost went out as he made his way up the stairs. He stopped for a moment as he felt a draft around him. He looked around. None of the windows were ajar, and he had already made sure that the doors were locked. So where was the breeze coming from? He shook his head and continued up the stairs. He must have been imagining the breeze. Maybe the cold had just gotten inside his bones. He had been out in the snow for quite a while that night, and the door slamming open had startled him a little. It must just be tonight's events making his imagination play tricks on him.

At the top of the stairs, he turned left and headed towards his bedroom when he heard footsteps behind him. He turned on the spot, his heart racing in anticipation. He hoped to see either Nora making her way to her room or one of the children up exploring the hall when they shouldn't be. But as he turned around, there was no one there. He lifted the candle high and low around him, but there was nothing to be seen in the dark hall before him except the orange glow of the candle flame.

He turned back in the direction of his room, trying to move as slowly and quietly as he could. His ears were ringing as they strained to focus on any small noise he might hear. All he could pick up was the faint padding of his own footsteps and the soft snow falling against the frosted windows. He tilted his head side to side, making each side of his neck crack before taking a deep breath and opening the door to his bedroom. The room was cold.

He shut the door behind him and headed to the fireplace, opposite his four-poster bed. Placing the candle on the mantelpiece, he bent down and balanced three logs on top of each other at slightly different angles. He stuffed some old newspaper between the coal and the spaces between the logs and lit it using the candle he was using for light. The newspaper burnt brightly and spread underneath the logs with a crackle. The room was soon filled with a warm glow from the fire, and slowly it started to feel a little more cosy.

Taking the candle away from the fireplace, he settled it on his bedside table and got ready for bed. Once in his night clothes, he climbed into bed and started reading his book as the fire crackled away. The front cover read, *'Discipline to the highest regard.'* There were a few other books that also lay on his table beside him, all again based on child discipline. *'Children are to be seen and not heard'*, *'Actions have consequences'*, and finally, *'Easy recipes for children'*.Obviously, he had been thinking about his stomach when he had picked this last book up.

It was quite evident that Mr. Hughes was always looking for new ways of disciplining the children and what else he could make them do. He surely was a lazy git. Not that he saw himself like that. He saw himself more as a god. He was giving children a home and food to eat. He was giving them an education. What more did they want?

He flicked through the pages, impressed by the way some of the actions in the book had been taken out. He took a pencil from the drawer next to him and started to underline a particular piece of text that spoke about how in Asia, they would punish the children by locking them in a small room and threatening them with ghosts. It was such a cruel act, but the thought of it made him smile.

As his pencil came to the end of the sentence, the fireplace blew out, as if a gust of wind had plummeted down the chimney and cast the flames out. He sat up straight in shock. It was still snowing outside, but looking out of his window, the trees stood motionless. No wind rustled their evergreen leaves. They stood idle, the moonlight glistening on the snow-covered branches.

The warmth that had filled the room from the fire seemed to have been sucked out, leaving the room freezing cold. He paced quickly to the fireplace, his hands shaking. He tried to relight the fire, but it was no use. No amount of paper would restart it, and as he tried to ignite the last piece of news parchment, the flame from his candle fizzled out.

He dropped the candle by the fireplace, and like a little schoolgirl, he jumped into bed. This once all-powerful man was frightened by the wind. Or was it the wind? He clutched the duvet cover, his eyes darting around the dark room. There was silence all around him. He squeezed his eyes tight and whispered to himself.

"Stop being so stupid, Toby. It's just the wind. It came down the chimney and extinguished the fire and did the same to the candle." But in his head, he remembered looking outside. There had been no wind.

"My Lord, please have no ill will against me. It was a mistake," he begged in whispers.

In the darkness of the room, a quiet little giggle could be heard.

"Who's there?" He shot up out of the bed, believing one of the girls was playing tricks on him. Not his Lord coming to punish him. "I demand you tell me your name!" he shouted.

Without any light, he tripped over the rug that lay beside his bed, and he seemed to fly through the air before he smacked his head on the solid wardrobe. Nora's room being next door, she had heard all the commotion and ran into his room.

"Toby, my goodness, are you okay? What happened?" she asked in a panic as she set her own candle beside him. Not wanting her to think he was childish or crazy, he didn't tell her about what had just happened. Instead, he lied.

"I was lying in bed thinking about how much you've helped me today and I wanted to repay you by making sure all the cakes were in a basket ready for when you left in the morning. So I got up, but the bloody rug had turned on itself and I tripped over the damned thing and hit my head on the bloody cupboard." He sat there rubbing his head.

"Get yourself back into bed. I'll run downstairs and get something to put on that bump of yours." Nora picked up her candle and relit Toby's so he could make his way back to bed. Nora made her way quickly downstairs to grab a rag to dampen and place on his head.

When she returned, Toby was fast asleep. The fall knocked all of his energy out of him. The candlelight flickered across his face, and she stood and stared at him, admiring every line, every mark on his face. He looked so peaceful. She laid the damp cloth on his forehead, placed the matches by his candle in case he wanted to light it in the night, and gently blew out the flame. She bent down, kissed him softly on his forehead, and with her fingers in the air, drew an invisible pentagram over the top of him.

"May the Lord protect you in your slumber, sweet sir." She headed back to her own room with her candle lighting the way.

That night he tossed and turned. Flashbacks of beating the little girl. Her pale face at the window screaming his name, transitioning to him burying her deep in the woods, her icy face taunting his dreams and laughing at him as he tripped over again and again. He thrashed around in the bed as he had visions of the little girl beating him. Getting her revenge for the beatings he gave her. The sound of the whip snapping against his skin made him scream. It was different when he whipped himself in ritual and worship. But to be whipped by a small child was emasculating. It was humiliating. Beads of sweat collected on his body and seeped into his bed sheets. When he awoke, he was lying in a puddle of smelly sweat. The bed stunk to the high heavens, his body odour filling the room from his violent night's sleep.

CHAPTER NINE
MOULD & CAKES

THE STORM CONTINUED throughout the day. The driveway now represented a lake that mirrored the flashes of lightning.

After the rug accident, Jenny decided to put the book to one side and indulge in more later. Right now, she remembered all the furniture that littered the basement floor and decided she wanted to check in there for another rug to replace the fire-scorched one next to her bed. She had already opened her window to let the smoky smell out, but the wind had driven in the rain, soaking the wooden floorboards.

As a result, not only did the room smell of burnt rug, it was cold and damp. She had just shut the window as a large gust of wind bellowed in, almost extinguishing the flames from the sizzling logs. Little did she know her attempt would be in vain.

The fire crackled loudly, with embers flickering up the chimney breast. The flames, after almost being diminished, were now an angry blaze. Jenny was in shock at the sight before her and didn't know what to do. She looked around in a panic. The rug! She grabbed the already scorched rug and started batting the fire ferociously in an attempt to quiet the ever-growing flames. Sweat dripped down her face as she continued to attack the fire. The heat in the room was becoming difficult to breathe through, causing a burning sensation in her lungs and her throat was screaming for moisture.

One massive gush of wind roared down the chimney with a force so strong, not only did it extinguish the flames, but also sent Jenny flying backwards, slamming her body into the foot of the bed, the back of her head smashing against the top edge of the hard oak. Her hand lightly brushed over the back of her skull, feeling a small bump forming there. She winced at the pain and the room around her began to spin.

Through her drunk-like vision, standing by the fireplace was a little girl. She looked frozen to the core, her lips blue as she stood trembling by the fire. She stared at Jenny, her eyes piercing with anger, not moving her gaze from the woman before her on the floor. She stepped slowly in Jenny's direction. Each step left small puddles where her icy body seemed to be melting from the warmth of the once ablaze fireplace. Jenny reached out to the girl as if pleading with her not to harm her. She was almost within reach, her hand about to touch her damp, dripping dress, when the child disappeared.

Her hand fell forward through the space where the little girl had stood. The mix of confusion and the knock to her head made her sick. She threw up next to the bed, just missing her mattress and sheets. She leant on the end of the bed to pull herself up, leaning her arm on the edge and her head rested on her arms for a moment, with closed eyes, as she tried to steady herself. She wiped her mouth, the horrid bile taste prevalent in her mouth.

As she opened her eyes, the world was still, and she noticed a crackling sound behind her. The fire had relit itself, the flames steady and the once damp floor now dry. It was as if the last few moments had never happened. Had she imagined it? Had she hallucinated the little girl by the fire? She lifted her hand to the back of her head in search of the painful lump, but it was also gone. There was no evidence of her hitting her head at all. What on earth had just happened? The only evidence she could find was the pile of vomit at the foot of the bed.

She walked into her en-suite, grabbed as many paper towels as she could hold, and mopped up the mess, when she heard a sinister giggle outside of her door. She stopped what she was doing. Unmoving and her hearing on full alert, she heard nothing. She dropped all the tissue, leaving a pile of vomit-soaked paper towels on the floor, and slowly made her way to her door, stepping lightly so as to not be heard.

Her hand gripped the round, brass handle. She closed her eyes, took a deep breath, and as she let the breath out, opened her eyes and twisted the doorknob. She opened the door ever so slightly, leaving a small gap in which she could see only one side of the lengthy hallway. Peering through, she could see no one there. Her heart was still racing at the thought that the ghostly child she had seen might be on the other side of the door just waiting for her. She couldn't just lock herself away in her room forever though. She swallowed the lump in her throat and gently opened the door, her fear growing as she stared into the hall.

She stepped into the dimly lit hall and a force rammed into her. Two screams echoed down the hallway at the same time as a loud rumble of thunder. Abigail had had her head in a book as she was walking back to her room from the library, and so wasn't looking where she was going she collided with Jenny, scaring them both to the bone.

"Sorry, Miss. I didn't see you," Abigail apologized.

"No, no, it's fine, Abigail. You just startled me is all. This storm doesn't want to give in, does it?" Jenny observed more than questioned.

"No Miss... Miss, are you okay? You don't look too well."

"I'm okay, just a little homesick, I suppose. What book do you have there?"

"Oh, just a book on ancient Greece. I love Greek mythology."

"Oh, the Greek gods! Fascinating subject." Jenny glimpsed at the title between the girls small fingers. It didn't seem to be on ancient Greece at all. In fact from what she could see on the cover it looked to be something on spells.

"The Greeks were into many different subjects weren't they? Many different Deities and ways of worshipping them."

"Yes, Miss." Abigail's eyes remained fixed to the floor instead of maintaining eye contact with her teacher.

"This is just for research isn't it Abigail? I wouldn't want you being involved with anything that may cause you any harm."

"Of course, Miss. What harm could come from reading about Greeks?"

"Of course, you're right," Jenny began, dismissing that Abigail could in fact do any harm. *Magic isn't real anyway right?*

"Well, I'll leave you to enjoy your book. Maybe wait to read it until you're back in your room though, avoid bumping into anyone else." Jenny smiled.

"Yes, Miss. Sorry again."

Abigail closed her book and continued down the hall. Before she was out of sight, Jenny noticed her book in her hands and she was already reading again as she made her way to her room.

Now that Jenny was in the hallway, she decided to head down to the basement and see if there was a spare rug hidden there. She held onto the handrail and stepped carefully and slowly down in the dark. The only light came from a small lamp at the bottom of the stairs and the flashes of lightning every few moments. She had left her candle in her bedroom, but she wasn't really in the mood to go back in there yet after what had just happened. Or at least, what she thought had just happened.

As she reached the bottom of the stairs, she stepped lightly over to the table and grabbed the lamp. With the lamp in hand, she headed down the hallway beside the stairs, remembering one of the planks that formed the wall needed pressing to reveal the doorway. She lifted the lamp close to the wood and scanned over the planks. On one, she noticed a dull, circular mark, a give-away that the area had been pushed time and time again and over the years had worn away slightly. She pressed her thumb into the indentation and the wood moved forward revealing a slot for a key.

"Damn it," she whispered. She had completely forgotten Lenora used a key to access the basement. Lenora had started creeping her out and Jenny really didn't want to bother her, especially after how weird she acted about the rug. Looking around to make sure the coast was clear, she took a pin from her hair and popped it in the lock. After a few twists and turns and hearing the right clicks, the door popped open.

She had learnt the technique from an old boyfriend. *What was it with her and choosing complete arseholes?* She had been a teen at the time, yet he was twice as old and a bad influence. She was drawn to his bad-boy approach to life. He was tall, had dark hair, and was muscular and fashioned a black leather jacket with worn faded denim jeans. He would take her out now and again on jobs. Not your normal nine-to-five jobs, but break-ins and robberies. His favourite was gold jewellery that he could pass off as a family heirloom and take to the local pawn shop for cash. Suffice it to say, he got caught and she never saw him again. She was heartbroken for months.

She popped her pin back in her hair, picked the lamp up from the floor, and let herself into the basement. The basement was in complete darkness, like the rest of the building, but the area under the stairs felt different somehow. It felt damp and decayed. No, not just felt, she could also smell it, the spores of something dead and rotten drifting into her lungs. She covered her nose with one hand in an attempt to block the smell, but it was no use. It had already crept in and lingered within her body, making her feel uneasy as she stepped down the foreboding staircase into the unknown.

The last time she had come down here was for a brief moment after explaining her dream to Lenora, when she saw the portrait of Mr Hughes. She had not explored it further due to the lights going out.

She continued into the blackness and lifted the lamp to illuminate the space around her. Black mould caressed the exposed brick of the surrounding walls, and tendrils of black gloop hung from the ceiling dripping inky water onto the concrete below. Surely, any furniture that remained down here would be ruined, already festering with the splattering black signs of damp, but she continued to look around anyway, not letting the stench deter her.

She kept herself away from the walls as much as she could, but it was crowded down there. Boxes that she assumed were filled with old belongings. The boxes themselves were falling apart from the moisture the cardboard had sucked in like a sponge. She could only imagine what the contents looked like, as she would rather not touch them. She weaved in-between stacked boxes and wooden chairs carefully balanced on one another.

There was a creak behind her as if someone had stepped on a loose floorboard. She twisted to face the sound, but as she turned the glass lamp smashed against the chairs, sending them toppling to the ground in front of her, along with the rest of the lamp, leaving just its handle in her grasp.

The darkness smothered her as she froze on the spot, letting the air still around her before she tried to make her way back to the steps. The sounds of dripping echoed through the dark shadows. Her eyes slowly started to adjust, no longer blind to her surroundings. She could make out shapes around her, and although she didn't want to be touching anything that may be saturated in mould, she had no other choice but to feel her way back toward her exit.

Not quick enough to snatch her hands away, her hands slid over wet boxes. The fast action to withdraw from the mouldy boxes sent her stumbling backward into more sodden boxes. She lay there in the squelching material, the smell piercing her nostrils. She desperately wanted to scream, but her throat enclosed it, not allowing its release.

Thoughts of the mould spreading from the cardboard onto her skin, encasing her as if being mummified in the black powder and goo, made her stomach tight, and a metallic taste formed underneath her tongue, making her want to retch. She rolled onto her side and opened her scrunched-shut eyes, only to meet with another's. This time her scream forced past the lump in her throat and adrenaline filled her body enough for her to run. She didn't care if she knocked things over or broke anything; she just wanted out.

Boxes went flying as she pushed them out of the way. She stumbled over smaller items on the floor but held herself up and got out as fast as she could. Her hand found the rail leading up the stairs and she ran, two steps at a time, until she was back in the hallway and the door was shut behind her. She rested up against the door, as if waiting for someone to try to escape or go after her. She leant against it hard, but no one came. The door stayed still and the only sounds echoing through the hallway were the rumbles of thunder still going strong outside. She waited there, letting her heart rate settle before she tried to move. Her legs felt like jelly and her hands were shaking.

In the dark hallway, she made her way to the kitchen, her hands holding onto the walls for support, not fully trusting her legs to hold her up. She pushed the dining room door open to find candles placed all along the tables and a sweet smell coming from the kitchen. She steadied herself as the odour filled her nose, shifting the previous smell that had been lingering in her nostrils. She could almost taste what had been cooking, a Victoria sponge, and it made her stomach grumble. But how had they cooked anything? They were in the midst of a power outage.

Motivated by the smell of food, Jenny made her way to the kitchen at the back of the dining room. She pushed the door open and it squeaked in reply.

"Oh, hello, dear," a flour-covered Lenora smiled. "What can I do for you? Lunch will be served shortly."

"You do all the cooking too?" Jenny asked.

"Yes, you won't find a better cook than myself, or a baker. Cakes are my speciality. Today's pudding is cake with summer fruits."

"It smells delicious. I was actually coming in here to find something sugary. I feel a little dizzy and thought some sugar might help." Jenny looked over to the oven, her tummy growling in hunger. The oven looked older than any she had ever seen before, and she definitely wouldn't be able to pick one up from her local appliance store.

"Of course, come sit down." Lenora pulled a stool out for Jenny to sit on whilst she ran to the fridge. "Here, try this," she said, handing Jenny a slice of pie. It was apple pie, with cinnamon in both the apple mixture and the crust. It also packed a little heat and Jenny couldn't work out why.

"This is delicious; what is the heat I'm getting?" she questioned, the taste completely distracting her from asking about the oven.

"Oh, that would be the ginger. You know, ginger is good for the stomach and helps relieve sickness. I add only a little as I don't want to overpower the taste from the apples and cinnamon."

"It's perfect," she said whilst stabbing another piece with her fork.

"So, what's made you feel unwell?"

"Nothing much really, I think everything is just catching up with me. You know, the ex." It wasn't the ex on her mind at all, but she couldn't really let slip that she had been nosing around in the basement. The basement which was locked and the key was hanging around Lenora's neck.

"I had a lover once. He was tall and handsome and loved my cakes."

"What happened?" she asked as she empathised with the woman covered in flour.

"He died." Her face dropped. "He was enchanting, so strong and manly. Always had my heart skipping a beat. I would have done anything for that man."

"What was his name?" But before Lenora could even answer, the dining hall door slammed open, making them both jump.

Jenny opened the kitchen door slightly and peered through into the candle-lit room. The flames flickered as if disturbed by something, or perhaps someone, although she couldn't see anyone in there. She pulled the door inwards and stepped into the large room. She slowly headed towards the tables when she noticed a shadow against the wall opposite her. Not knowing whether it was a trick of the light or if there was someone there, she grabbed one of the candles from the nearest table and small step after small step made her way toward the shadow.

"It's probably just the wind, Jenny," Lenora called out to her quietly. She ignored her. One slow step after the other, she continued forward in silence. The door took her by surprise and slammed shut, a gust of wind howled around the room, extinguishing every flame that gave her light, including the one she was clutching.

CHAPTER TEN
DEATH BED

"JESUS CHRIST!" TOBY WAS FREAKING OUT and really didn't care he was using blasphemy. He was no lord of *his,* so what did it matter? To him, the real Lord was the one *he* worshipped. Nights dedicated to praying at his alter and days to make sure the children did the same. Early morning prayers were done at their bedsides before starting their daily chores — these came before breakfast.

His dreams caused him to thrash about all night, but sweat had saturated his bed sheets and his smell lingered in the air. It was thick and musky.

His room happened to be the only one with an en-suite shower, of which, of course, had hot water. The water the girls had to use was from the well outside and cold. Even the other staff didn't have the privilege of hot water. But he didn't care, why would he? As long as he was comfortable, that's all that mattered.

His way of looking at it was that he was the Lord's right-hand man. He kept a roof over their heads. He paid for the food that went into their bellies. So why *shouldn't he* have had the only access to the luxury of hot water? He worked with his Lord and had been rewarded with money to use as he wished. A relative of his had died and left him a sizeable inheritance, yet he believed it was the powers of his dark Lord that had caused the man to die, thus leaving him the money. He used it on luxuries he couldn't otherwise afford— like the shower.

He flung the drenched top sheet to the floor, revealing his naked, sweaty body. Sweat still rolled off his skin, from where his curly chest hair lay flat on his body and onto the thin mattress. What startled him even more was the brown filth that had mixed in with his sweat.

The sheet was stained and looked like a wet, filthy dog had been rolling around in it. He squirmed at the sight and jumped from his bed in shock. He slowly brushed his fingers over the thick substance he had laid in to find it had a muddy consistency. It was dirt. But how? When he went to bed there were no signs of dirt on him from where he had buried Sylvie. His clothes were drenched from the snow and dripping onto the floor from the chair where he had laid them, but no signs of earth had lingered on himself or his clothing.

He screwed up the dirt-infected sheet and placed it with his other sheets, throwing them into the corner for one of the children to pick up and wash later. He strolled into the shower room, putting the soiled sheets to the back of his mind, and twisted the shower knob. The handle screeched as he kept twisting it. No water flowed from overhead. Frustration bubbling up inside him like a kettle, he whacked the knob with his fist, his eyes staring up at the shower head, waiting for it to spring into action.

"Useless dratted thing. Work!" he shouted. And just as the words left his mouth, the water blasted right into his face, causing him to jump backward, hitting his hip on one of the cage-like pipes.

Cursing under his breath, he let the steam fill up the tiny room and admired himself in the mirror on the back of the door. He turned his face side to side, noticing his strong jawline, and smiled. He saw himself as a good-looking man, a man women found desirable. He flexed his arm muscles and smiled to himself before stepping under the flow from the shower.

He let out a harrowing scream as he leapt back out from under the water. He was expecting a nice warm shower when he stepped in. Instead, icy water shot out, stinging his leg with a sharp bite.

"Mr Hughes?" a little voice called into the room. One of the girls had knocked on the door to collect his washing. She peered in shyly. Hearing the running water, she picked up his sheets bundled on the floor, but was startled as she heard Mr Hughes scream. She instantly dropped the overpowering smelly bundle and ran over to the shower-room door and banged on it several times.

"Mr Hughes? Mr Hughes, are you alright?"

He was not. His leg had a scorch burn on his leg. But it was no burn, at least not a hot one. It was an ice burn. It had formed a ring on his shin, making it cracked and sore, and was so pale it almost looked blue.

"Get in here, girl!" he shouted after pulling the towel from the door hook to cover himself. "Get me up and back to my bed. Then get Miss Nora," he demanded.

The young girl swooped in next to Mr Hughes and he placed his arm over her small shoulders without even looking at her. She hated the feel of his cold, wet skin pressed up against her. He was almost naked and had his arm around her. She prayed silently that his towel remained around his thick waist.

"Are you sure you don't want me to send for a nurse?" she questioned, then wished she never had.

"Shut up you silly girl. Just get Miss Nora, she will know what to do."

She struggled to get him over and onto his bed, but as she sat him on his stained mattress, he looked at her face and froze.

"Y-y-y-you! But…" He closed his eyes and shook his head, opening them to a different face. The one he first saw was little Sylvie, he was sure of it. But looking at her now, she was different. Not Sylvie at all.

"Are you okay, sir?"

"GET NORA!" he shouted.

She ran from the room, careful not to trip over his stinking sheets, slammed his door behind her, and left the unstable man alone in his room. *What was happening? Was he losing it? He did have a few drinks the night before, was it just an illusion provoked by whiskey?* He laid back on his sheetless mattress. Although the sheets were gone, he could still smell the sweat and mud. It was rancid. He closed his eyes for a few seconds to rest before they shot back open. He could hear a child laughing; in his head, the child was laughing at him. Laughing at him for sweating through the night after having nightmares, laughing at him for having scorched his leg in freezing water. Someone was toying with him, and he didn't find it funny.

"Who's there?" he shouted from his bed. He got no reply, yet he could still hear the child's giggle. Was it one or more? He thought he could hear more than one voice laughing at him, but he couldn't be certain. It was almost like an echo of the first laughter.

"I demand you to enter my room!" he shouted. The doorknob twitched to the right and then fully turned to the left until it clicked. It creaked open slowly until the hallway was in clear view and it hit against the wall. Nobody entered and no one was standing in the doorway waiting to go in.

"Who's... out there?" This time when he questioned, he was nervous. He swallowed hard around the lump forming in his throat. If there wasn't anyone there, then what was? The window next to his bed sounded as though it had cracked. When he looked there was no crack at all. Instead, ice was forming slowly up the window, covering it in pretty patterns as if flowers were being painted with ice. The air around him became cooler and his breath turned into clouds before him. He shivered with just his towel around his waist for warmth.

The icy patterns spread like veins around the walls of the room, covering them in a sparkly frost. A wind blew around the room, slamming his door closed just as the ice started to spread over its hinges, and caused the door to freeze shut. He was trapped.

Trapped in his own snow globe of a room. The ice was spreading across the floor and surrounding him, coming closer and closer. Trapping him on his bed.

The pain in his shin became more piercing, and his hands shot to the frozen area, pleading for the pain to ease, praying to the Lord for blood to return to his frostbitten wound.

He screamed out in pain as icy fingers projected from the floor and spread over his bare feet. He lashed himself backward on the bed, retrieving his feet from the icy hands reaching up to him. As he fell backward on his cold mattress, he glimpsed a face in the iced patterns on his window. A child. A tear seemed to fall from her ice-painted eye, down the frozen pane, and onto his bed. This was not the only droplet, but the first of many.

DRIP. DROP. DRIP.

Little drips padded down onto his bed and his bare skin, one falling onto his clammy forehead. He looked up. Plumes of his breath were visible, but that didn't stop him from seeing through them. Above, hanging from the top of his four-poster bed, were thick, sharp icicles that hung over his body. Droplets trickled down their icy points, and before he even had a chance to move, the one above his head broke free and plummeted straight through his gawping, screaming mouth, the shard so strong and pointed it impaled his throat and pinned him to the mattress below.

"Toby? What's wrong? Anna said you'd hurt your leg. I'm sorry I took so long, I just dealt with Nancy. She won't be a problem now," Nora said, pushing the door open with ease.

The room was as it had originally been. Completely clear of any ice, with no icicles threatening to impale, no sparkling frost around the walls, and no ice rink flooring. Just his usual, plain room.

Nora noticed Toby laying on the bed and made her way over to him, passing the sheets that had been left in a bundle to the side. She scrunched up her nose as the dank body odour flew inside her nostrils. She hoped Toby hadn't noticed her expression.

"What have you…" She stopped, frozen, just as the room was only moments before. Toby lay still in his literal death bed. His frost-bitten leg was the only evidence of injury to his body. Her eyes focused on the frozen meat of his leg before meeting with his eyes. She gasped in horror and her steps retreated from his bedside. His eyes, once alive and bright with colour, were white and both irises were a frosty shade of pale blue with no pupils to be seen. Frost laced his eyelashes, giving an enchanted frame to his glassy eyes.

She was rooted to where she stood, in shock at the scene before her. She wanted to scream, but her voice was trapped by her tongue being forced to the back of her throat, causing her to hold her breath out of shock. Her heart was pounding against her chest. A solitary tear welled up in her eye, threatening to escape with just one blink, as she stared blankly at his lifeless body. She could feel herself going numb and the world around her blurring out of existence as she fell to her knees. She blinked once, that one tear making its escape down her cheek, before she collapsed to the ground. Her eyes open, staring blankly into nothingness as she lay there, her knees pulled tight up to her chest.

"He's just the start," a threat whispered to her, and although she didn't see it, a child's handprint slid down the icy window. Adrenalin pumping through her veins, she sat up in fear. "And _you_ won't be the last."

She stumbled to her feet as fast as her body was able and darted out of the room and down the stairs to the hall. She flung the doors open, wailing,

"He's dead. She killed him. He's dead!"

"Who's dead? Nora, what's going on?" The cook rushed over to Nora, who once again was on her knees sobbing her heart out.

"Tobias! He's dead! And there's only one person not here today."

"Oh my god! Nancy? She couldn't have! Could she? Why would she? Where is Mr Hughes now?" She couldn't get the questions out quickly enough.

"He's in his room, on his bed."

Turning around to see who was closest to her, the cook called out, "Elizabeth, send for the police."

Elizabeth ran from her seat and into the hallway, out of sight.

"She killed him, I know she did," Nora sobbed, knowing full well Nancy hadn't killed him at all. She had spent the early hours of the morning at Nancy's house.

It was a small, stone cottage. About an hour's walk away, so Nora had woken early to make her way there. She had popped her head in through Toby's door to make sure he was okay before she left. And he had been; well, he had at least been alive, as she saw him tossing and turning under his bed sheet.

Nancy lived just on the outskirts of the village, so no one really spoke to or saw her. At that time, in the early morning, no one would have seen Nora visiting Nancy. She was surprised to see Nora at her front door in the early morning rain. She opened the door and rushed Nora inside, away from the dreary morning outside. The only good thing to come from the rain was that at least the snow was melting from the paths, and Nora hoped not to walk back to Eden through the snow-covered ground.

She shook off her coat. The splatters of rain that saturated Nora's coat dripped onto Nancy's wooden floor, leaving a small puddle as it dried off on the coat rack. Stepping into the heart of the room, she placed the baked goods on the kitchen table.

Nancy was just getting ready for her day at Eden Orphanage, the unsettling image of Sylvie's dead body in the snow still fresh in her mind. The small, crackling fire kept the space warm against the cold trying to break in through the single-pane windows.

"Miss Nora, is everything okay?" she asked, worried as to why she was there so early, or as to why she was there at all.

"Oh yes, yes, dear. I was coming around early to catch you before you came in. Mr Hughes has suggested you have the next few days off after the fright you had last night. Not a nice thing to see. The police will be looking into what happened, but we seem to all agree that she must have snuck out whilst we were all busy with our evening chores and preparing for dinner. We cannot think of how else this may have happened. Lord knows what the child was doing out in the freezing cold, especially without the correct clothing. Perhaps squeezing in some play time in the snow, but she really should have asked. No one is at fault in this case. We only wish she had come to us before going out there, or at least had someone with her."

"That poor girl. I wish I had found her sooner. I don't even know how she got out. All the doors were locked. She shouldn't have been able to get out there. Not unless someone…"

Nora interrupted before she could finish her sentence. She knew exactly what Nancy was about to say and thought to put an end to the conversation quickly, before she got any ideas.

"Here, darling, I baked you some cakes. It's the least I can do after all your hard work and what you've been through." She whipped the fabric from the top of the cakes and slid the basket over to Nancy. "I baked them last night as soon as Toby informed me. Thought they would cheer you up."

"Oh, thank you, Nora. They smell delicious." She picked up a small cupcake, still in its paper case, and let the fresh-baked smell fill her nose.

"I know lavender cake is your favourite," Nora smiled. "Go on, have a bite. It's never too early for cake."

Nancy folded down the paper wrapper, fluffy crumbs falling to the floor, and stuck her teeth through the lavender-laced icing and into the fragrant sponge of the cake. The taste of vanilla and lavender mixed in her mouth with the soft sponge, disguising anything else Nora may have placed inside it.

"Oh, Nora, these are divine," she said with her mouth half full.

Nora made her way over to one of the cupboards above the counter space and opened the rickety door. She grabbed a glass and headed to retrieve the milk bottle from the icebox. She was lucky that before her uncle died he had the money to install one for her. Everyone else in the village had to make do with cellars. Not even Eden Orphanage had an icebox! Although, as it was so cold outside, an icebox probably wasn't needed right now.

"Here," she said, filling the glass with the icy cold liquid. "You can't beat a glass of milk with a cupcake."

Nancy stuffed the last of her cupcake in her mouth before gulping down some milk.

"Not to be greedy, but these are scrumptious." she said, grabbing another cake from the basket. "You must give me your recipe."

And just like that, another idea sprung to Nora's mind.

"Of course! Have you paper and a quill? I can note it down now for you." This could not be going better if she tried! Now it would definitely look as though Nancy had baked them herself. The list of ingredients and baking method would be sitting on her countertop and no one would bat an eyelid! She wrote out the list on the small piece of paper Nancy had found in a drawer and placed it next to the cakes for her.

"Thank you, Nora. I will have to bake some for my cousin's wedding next year." Nancy picked up another, not being able to stop herself from devouring her favourite cake.

"You are more than welcome," she replied, turning away to hide her sinister smile.

Nancy's hand reached for her stomach slowly, the last of her second cake still in her mouth. A frown appeared across her forehead, confused by the sudden pain growing in her abdomen. She had noticed a dull ache beforehand, but within seconds the pain intensified. Now sharp pains caused her to double over.

She leant against the table in pain whilst a heat started to spread through her throat. Her other hand reached up to cover her mouth as she spluttered the remaining contents of her cupcake onto the table. Heat spread throughout her body, and she began to feel wheezy and sick. Sweat trickled down her ashen face. Nancy fell to her knees, no longer able to hold herself up against the strength of gravity pulling her weak, burning body to the floor. Her hand was still hovering over her mouth as a mix of blood and bile came spewing from inside her, covering herself and the floor and just missing Nora. Nora stepped back, away from the bloody mess that had erupted from Nancy. She continued to keep her eyes fixed on Nancy as she convulsed and suffered before her on the floor.

Her throat became constricted, as if someone had their hands around it, tightening and squeezing, the heat in there becoming more intense. Her throat had swollen so much that Nancy could barely breathe. On her hands and knees, her body trembling, she reached out to Nora for help, her lips turning blue.

Nora stepped away from her reach and turned to make sure the kitchen side was prepped for when anyone eventually found her. In the bottom of her basket, she had hidden a small bag of flour and scattered it over the side and floor. She grabbed the list of ingredients and scrunched it up slightly, making it look as though Nancy had had the recipe for some time, all the while completely ignoring Nancy's pleas for help before she finally perished.

Nora placed the rest of the cakes in a few small lines, as if they had been left to cool. The scene now set, Nora picked up her umbrella and basket and stepped back out into the miserable, dark morning. She placed her umbrella before her into the rain to make sure it covered her and she set forward, back to the orphanage, minus the deadly cupcakes.

CHAPTER ELEVEN
THE UNKNOWN

JENNY STOOD IN THE DARK hall, every one of the candles now extinguished. The smell of smoke and melted wax floated on the air. She couldn't even make out the plumes of breath that came from her mouth as the air froze around her. The hairs on her arms stood up on end like needles of fear upon her skin.

Her surroundings were the same whether she had her eyes open or closed; her sight would not adjust to the lack of light. Her other senses had, however, peaked. Her hearing was more defined and her nose became more sensitive than a bloodhound's, picking up on even the slight smell of dusty surfaces.

A small click behind her indicated Lenora had locked the kitchen door. Whether that was to protect herself out of fear or to trap Jenny in the hall she was unsure, but she remained glued to where she stood. Light footsteps seemed to travel from the entrance of the hall. Step after step headed in her direction, around the outside of the dinner tables that sat idle. She stepped back, as if it would make a difference. Where could she escape to? The kitchen was locked, and the noise came from the other side of the room, where the other doors were. No escape and nowhere to hide. She tried as much as she could to put on a brave face and stand up to whoever or whatever had been approaching her in the dark.

"Who's there?" she called out to the unknown entity teasing her with their footsteps. There was no reply from whatever was taunting her, but a disgusting smell approached her, smothered the insides of her nose, and caused her to gag. It was a mixture of sulphur and what she could only imagine a decaying body would smell like. Putrid and sickening. The smell threw her off guard and she lost track of where the footsteps had been approaching.

The sounds had stopped. She found it hard to pinpoint the being's location. There was nothing but silence and the awful rotten smell invading her senses. She stepped back towards the kitchen in hopes of its safety with Lenora.

"Lenora, what's going on?" she called through the kitchen door. The door was still firmly locked as she pushed on the handle. The handle's rattle echoed through the hall. "Let me in!" she begged. Lenora didn't answer, nor did she unlock the kitchen door.

A loud smash broke the silence of the room. Without light, she couldn't make out what had broken or what had caused it to break. She couldn't remember if there had been any decorations in the hall or if there had been any plates laid out for when lunchtime came around. The smashes came one after the other, getting closer and closer to where she stood desperately shaking the handle on the kitchen door.

The air around her was icy cold, like a wall of ice entrapping her at the end of the hall, with no way to escape. She crumbled to the floor, placing her arms over her head, and screamed. The sound of her piercing voice echoed through the hall and the rest of the school.

"Jenny! What's wrong? Are you okay?" Lenora came bounding through the hall's entrance and ran to where Jenny was curled up in a ball on the floor.

Jenny opened her eyes and lifted her head. The hall was filled with candlelight. There was no sign of anything being damaged.

"Why wouldn't you let me in? Why did you lock me in here?" she cried.

"Jenny, what are you talking about? The doors were open. I was in my room marking papers when I heard you scream."

"No… No. I came in here feeling unwell and you were getting lunch ready in the kitchen. You gave me some food to help with my nausea. Then something was in here, in the hall. You locked me in here with no light and someone was taunting me. Who was it? Why did you do that? Is this some sort of newcomer game? If it is, it's not very funny."

"Jenny, I think you're even more ill than you think." Lenora looked towards the door. Many of the children were gathered there, all holding their own candles, and most of them looked afraid. "Let's get you up to your room. I will personally bring your lunch to you. I'll make you some chicken and lemongrass soup with ginger."

Jenny was sure that ginger helped with nausea, so Lenora was clearly trying to help her. At least, she hoped so. She remembered the cake that Lenora had given her in the kitchen. She hadn't imagined it at all. *Why is she lying to me?* Trying to make sense of it all caused her head to hurt and made her feel sick once again.

"Why are you lying to me?" Jenny questioned aloud, stepping away from Lenora.

"Jenny, if I had locked you in and kept myself in the kitchen, how did I just come through the hall entrance?"

Jenny looked back at the kitchen door and then over to the entrance. She rushed over to the kitchen and twisted the handle. As before, the kitchen door was still locked. No one was inside the kitchen, nor had anyone stepped in there since breakfast.

"Then how…" Jenny couldn't finish the sentence. She stood there in a confused daze. She was sure she hadn't imagined the last few moments. It was so vivid she could still smell the lingering death inside her nostrils. She couldn't be imagining that as well, could she?

"Maybe this was too much all at once for you, Jenny. Leaving your first school, your breakup with your fiancé, and straight into

84

a new job. It was all very rushed." Lenora sighed with empathy. "Look, I can plan things for the girls to do for the rest of the day. Head up to bed and rest, I'll bring you some soup."

Jenny had no words. She was dumbstruck. She nodded and made her way toward the hall doors. The girls all parted to make way for her. Abigail passed her candle to Jenny.

"Miss, here, take my candle. It's dangerous in the dark without it."

She seemed to give Jenny a weird look as she passed the candle to her. Her eyes stared sharply into hers, almost as though she was worried for her. Did Abigail know what was happening? Had she not imagined it after all? There was definitely something strange going on here. Jenny lingered a moment longer than what would have been seen as normal. She stared into Abigail's eyes, trying to work out her expression with her own look of confusion as she took the candle from Abigail's hands. There was no holder for this candle. The hot wax had been trickling down its length and onto poor Abigail's hand, now doing the same to Jenny's.

"Thank you," Jenny said softly, trying to ignore the sting from the molten wax. As much as she wanted to, she didn't ask Abigail why she had looked at her that way or what she had meant when she said about it being dangerous in the dark. She was afraid of looking even more insane than she had already been made out to be. Instead, she accepted the candle and made her way down the corridor and up the stairs. This candle felt strange in her hand.

Beneath her fingertips, she felt jagged markings branded into the wax. She hadn't held any of the other candles like this, as she had always found them sitting in a holder she could carry as she walked about. She knew better than to look whilst she was still surrounded by the children.

Their eyes were glued to her every step until she was out of sight. Something didn't sit right with Jenny. She hadn't imagined what had just happened. The dark. The thing in the dark. Lenora. *What is she hiding? And why did she just lie directly to my face? I need to find out what is going on here. No teachers, only a dozen or so children. I'm not even sure there are any other*

85

*staff. What's the real reason they got me in? I need to find out…
but how?*

When she was back in her room, she lit her own candle and
blew the one out in her hand. She picked at the wax that had
formed little mounds and waxy veins on her hands and then
turned her attention to the candle Abigail had handed her.

There was an upside-down pentagram symbol branded on the
surface, which seemed to be filled with a dark red substance. It
was dry and flaky as she scratched at it. The worst thought she
could think came to her mind. Blood. It couldn't be, could it?
Why would the candles have blood-soaked upside-down
pentagrams? She placed her hand around the lit candle on her
bedside table and wriggled it out, its flame flickering as she did
so. It had the same markings.

Jenny was becoming more and more freaked out by the
second.

"Calm down, Jenny," she whispered to herself in reassurance,
whilst staring at the candles in her hands. She placed them back
on the table, her hands slightly shaking. "Come on now. Plan of
action. Think."

She grabbed her bag from under the bed. She hadn't been able
to bring much because she had left home before thinking about
what she would really need; she had been too in shock. She
remembered her laptop in her bag, and it should still have a little
charge left. She pulled the laptop out and popped it onto the bed
beside her and pressed the on button. The laptop fired up, but it
was so slow. She grabbed the dongle that gave her internet access
and pushed it into the USB slot on the side of the laptop. A
message popped up on her screen.

NO SERVICE AVAILABLE.

What do you mean 'no service available?' She unplugged the
USB stick and forced it back in.

"Oh, come on you stupid thing! Work! Please!" she begged as
she stared at the screen impatiently. As she shoved the stick back
into the laptop for the final time, and the web page sprung to life.
The signal bar at the bottom of the page was showing a very

weak signal, so she typed as quickly as she could. *Please just let me find something before the signal goes. Please!*
She typed the name of the school into the search engine. A few links popped up in her search, but she couldn't find the same link she had come across in her initial search. The day she had driven away from her fiancé there was a school web page and a detailed job opportunity.
Her job.
Now, the page was non-existent. There were no details on how to contact the school or any information to show it was still a working school.
She continued to the links below.

Eden Orphanage.
Old Eden School History.
Old Eden School to close permanently.

Her eyes froze on the last link. *But I've only just arrived, and no one has ever mentioned the school was going to shut down. Is that why there are no teachers? But why would they have employed me just to take the job away from me again?* A million questions formed in her head.
She clicked the link. Surely it was a hoax. Someone had made up a silly rumour and plastered it on the internet. They must have. The page flashed before her. It was an article talking about the events that led to the decision for the school closure. But, it also stated the date. 02-Oct-1951. *What? But... how? Had the school closed back then and reopened? I know they said they were permanently closed, but maybe circumstances had changed.*
She continued to read through the article to find out why they had shut in the first place. She had decided that once she had read the report, she would then discuss it with Lenora. She was the school historian after all, so she should know about the school's history.

As of the 15th of October, Old Eden School For Girls will be closing after the death of 13-year-old Abigail Gleeves.

The school has been notorious for girls going missing, and several deaths have occurred on the premises dating back to when the school was an orphanage.

There have been many claims as to why these event occurred. Some say there is a murderer or kidnapper that has been on the loose for decades and has never been caught, but there are also those that believe the school has its very own curse.

Whether you believe in the paranormal or you think this is down to something more human, the school has become a very dangerous place for young girls to be educated.

It has not just been young girls to have gone missing; some of the staff have also disappeared. Again, it has never been confirmed, nor any detail substantiated, but what is clear is these people were never seen again.

A statement from the police has confirmed that no bodies of staff members have ever been found, and as a result, they believe the staff members have moved on.

They had no comment on the children that had also gone missing.

Our thoughts are with the parents and families of those young children taken too soon.

Lenora had been right about one thing, the children going missing and the deaths, but she had said it was a problem in the area, not just the school and she had never informed Jenny of the school closure. *Why didn't she tell me about the school closing? What is she hiding?*

Wanting to find out more, she clicked back onto the search engine and looked for the link about the history of Eden Orphanage. She scrolled down to the link and clicked. Her screen flashed in time with the forked lightning outside her window and faded into darkness. *No! Oh, come on!* Jenny tapped on multiple buttons on the keypad in hopes something would bring the screen back to life. Nothing worked, and out of aggravation she slammed the laptop lid shut.

"Well, now what?" she huffed. Without her laptop and internet, she had no idea how she was going to find out more information. She was sure, however, that Lenora was not going to give up all the information that she wanted. She rubbed her hands over her face in frustration and let out a big breath.

If it wasn't for the dreadful storm outside, she would have headed to the next village to see if they had a library. They would have definitely been able to help her. She loved the library where she used to live. It was the biggest around for miles, with beautiful Gothic features and high arched ceilings with rows and rows of books on all topics. It was a real-life Disney library. The staff there were always kind enough to help with anything she was researching for her class. *I wonder what they would think if I was to go in and ask for help on this.* She chuckled to herself. She knew that if someone had come to her asking the questions she was wanting to ask, she would either think they were in danger or losing the plot. More than likely the latter.

She was distracting herself from the main issue. *I need to get information. Abigail had hinted to me that something wasn't right. I'm sure of it. Maybe I can speak to her in private.*

Lenora tapped on the door three times before opening the door a crack.

"Jenny? Are you awake?" She waited outside the door for Jenny to answer. She had half expected for Lenora to walk right in as she had done previously.

"Yes, come in," she replied as she sat down on her bed. The rain beat against her window and the thunder continued to rumble.

"Here, this should make you feel better." Lenora placed a tray on the bed next to Jenny. It held a bowl of steaming soup, a bread roll, and a glass of orange juice.

"I've added a small amount of turmeric and ginger to your orange juice too. It will really help get you back in ship shape. It's packed full of vitamins, both the drink and the soup."

"Thank you, Lenora, and sorry for my outburst. You're probably right. I've been trying to ignore recent events and focus on work, but it hasn't done me any good. I really need to come to terms with what's happened. It's no good just bottling everything up," Jenny lied.

Of course, it's not good to bottle things up, but she wasn't sorry for what had happened that day and she didn't have an outburst. She was being lied to, but she couldn't let on to anything yet.

"I was wondering if I could ask you something?" Jenny started, not quite sure whether she should, but her mouth was quicker than her brain.

"Go on," Lenora replied.

"When I looked up the school as I was on my way here, I came across something that said the school had once closed down. I ignored it thinking they must have been speaking about another school and wondered if you could tell me if it was this school or another?" She already felt in her gut that she wouldn't get the answer she wanted, She knew she had lied about finding the information before arriving there, but she couldn't let on that she knew something wasn't quite right.

"No dear, why on earth would the school be shut down? I have worked here for years without any worry of it being closed."

"Oh, I just remembered you saying about the people that had gone missing the other day when you showed me around, so I thought maybe that had been a cause for the school to close."

"Oh no, dear. As I said before, these things happen in this area. No one knows why or what happened to them." *Liar. Why was she still lying? What the hell was she hiding?*

"Hmm, okay," she smiled, not letting on that she knew otherwise. "I wonder if it was a murderer… oh, what if it was the old guy. You know, the one who owned the orphanage," Jenny joked, but she was nervous inside. Was she pushing too far?

"Don't be absurd!" The bitter words spat from Lenora's mouth. "Sorry, but it's something one of the children would come up with and start spreading silly rumours. They probably ran off; you know what kids are like, always running away."

Jenny was completely taken aback, not expecting Lenora to burst into anger so suddenly. *What is it about that man and her? Were they once related or something?*

"Sorry, I didn't mean for you to take offence. Was he a relative of some sort?" she dared to question.

"No. I just admire what he did for the children. Instead of them fending for themselves in a time of war, he kept a roof over their heads, educated them, and took them to church every Sunday without fail."

She didn't fool Jenny in the slightest. She knew there was more to it than that. Her mind went back to the library. Of course! There's a library in the school!

"I understand,." Jenny's lips softened to hide her true feelings. "Speaking of education, I was talking to Abigail earlier about books that she was interested in. I wonder if you could send her in. I would love to speak to her more on the subject. She is a very smart little spark."

"Of course, but are you sure? I'm certain she won't have too much to say. She is an awfully quiet child."

"Yes, please. I feel she can open up to me more if we talk about books. I was very much a book nerd growing up, too, so I feel we can relate to one another."

"I'll send her in then. Make sure to eat your soup. We need you healthy. Can't run the school on my own now, can I?" She smiled at Jenny, although it came across sarcastically as she spoke the words. Jenny didn't reply but gently picked up the tray and placed it on her lap. She plunged the spoon into the warm soup and started eating.

CHAPTER TWELVE
LAST LEAP

NORA WAS LOST IN HER OWN HEAD for the rest of the morning and into the afternoon. It was as if her head space was now an empty shell. Four solid walls encased her in a dark, lonely cell. She was numb.

Silent tears fell from bloodshot eyes. The pools that filled her eyes stung like acid until the substance made its escape to the cell's concrete floor, where it was soaked up like a sponge. The more she cried, the more tears were sucked into the crevices and turned into a black gloop. The black sludge seeped through the stone walls of her empty cell and dropped from the ceiling that had already turned black. It covered the space like a toxic mould dripping around her, filling the windowless box. The ooze flooded her brain, smothering every thought that had been residing in the evil pit of her head.

She sat in a daze, her brain not functioning and her body not responding to anyone or anything. She had run from Mr Hughes' bedroom and alerted everyone. Elizabeth had rushed to get help as instructed, but Nora then fell silent, as if all the life had unexpectedly been sucked out of her. She was just a vessel. No words, no actions, no expressions, not even a twitch. She just sat on the cold stone floor motionless.

The wind outside was howling and forcing a gale of hailstones into the windows that surrounded the hall. Even the noise of the hail battering the building hadn't phased her as the sound grew louder, echoing through the building and bouncing back off each stone wall.

A pair of white eyes appeared in her gloop-flooded cell. The sticky substance started to drain from her mind, and around the white stony eyes, the rest of the apparition started to form. Glazed golf balls sat in sunken sockets, translucent skin showing purple and blue veins laced with flakes of frost.

Her body was surrounded by shadows once the black substance drained away. She moved slowly, as if the frost had eaten through her skin into her bones, forcing them to crack as she moved inwards. Her image grew bigger and bigger until just her face filled the shadowy cell of Nora's brain. The girl's eyes didn't blink, didn't move. Eyes once full of colour, now even the dark pupils were hazed over. Eerily she stayed there unmoving, like a statue, until a sharp scream left the girl's mouth, filling Nora's head and piercing her ears.

Nora's body, still sitting in the hall, mimicked the girl in her brain. Her head snapped backward and she let out a horrific scream that silenced the hail beating the windows around her. Staff ran in from every corner of the building, hands firmly clasped over their ears as they ran towards her. Many stopped short after entering the hall, seeing her body starting to twist.

Her head was still forced back as if looking at the ceiling, her jaw as wide open as it could possibly get, but it must have dislocated given the angle it was now sitting in. Her arms were twisted into awkward angles that caused her joints to be out of their usual position. The sight was frightening to onlookers, and the staff were having to get the children back to the dorm.

A few stayed behind with Nora's contorted, screaming body. Nora finally fell silent but remained in her awkward position. One girl who worked in the kitchen had been sitting by her. She hesitantly removed her hands from her ears and gingerly reached forward to touch Nora's arm. Nora was frozen, her skin ice cold, but the woman's fingers burned through the icy layer. A scorching sensation seeped through Nora's nerve endings and the scream once again pierced the ears of every person in the room.

The woman's body was thrown backward in shock as the scream invaded her ears. As she lay on her back, she noticed something lingering in the shadows on the ceiling above Nora. Two eyes were focused on her as if staring into her very soul. She looked up at her in disbelief, unable to move from the shock of what she was seeing. The eyes shifted to her petrified gaze. She tried to get up and run, but before she had time to gain her balance, a force exploded through the hall, sending everyone crashing to the ground with screams and gasps.

The energy, unwilling to let them move, froze their bodies to the stone floor. Ice encased their screaming bodies, creating sparkling, frosted sculptures from the people that had failed her in life. Sylvie was out for revenge and wouldn't stop until every person who failed her was dead. Everyone was going to pay!

She floated from the shadows on the ceiling down to her glacial masterpiece. She walked amongst the ice statues throughout the hall before reaching Nora. She placed a hand on Nora's body. She was not completely frozen like the rest of the bodies in the room. Her skin was cold to the touch and frosty, but she was still alive. Sylvie wanted to drag this torture out. She had to pay for all the ill-treatment she had caused, and Sylvie was not about to make things easy for her. With her hand placed on top of Nora's head, she started an incantation.

"A curse to all who failed me in life.

A curse to their families no matter the husband or wife.

This curse shall remain through to *HIS* last heir.

This way I see to be only fair.

Mr Hughes and those who sided with him will remain grounded in this icy grave.

Only after his last remaining child's death will you be saved."

She threw her arms out and a force shock-waved through the entire building, windows were blown into shards of glass, and any remaining person in the building was thrown against walls or out through the glassless panes. The only body left alive was Nora's. Sylvie took her hand off Nora's head and vanished. Nora's body collapsed to the ground.

When she regained consciousness, she had no idea what had happened whilst she was under Sylvie's control. Her eyes blinked open to see other bodies around her. Her body, aching and stiff, made her move slowly. She pushed up off the cold, stone floor and lifted her head as she knelt on her knees. Looking around she felt horror strike her very soul — dark as it was, she surprisingly still had one.

The bodies around her were icy and solid. Not one person blinked. They were the result of Sylvie's revenge. She had turned them all to ice. Tears flooded Nora's eyes as she realised what must have happened. The tears dropped onto the frozen surface below her and turned to ice. She tried to stand, but the surface was so slippery she lost her balance and fell against one of the women encased in ice. The form shattered as she fell into it, sending pieces of frozen flesh all around.

The horror surrounding her forced adrenaline to charge through her body. In her attempts to run and escape the horrific scene, she slipped and stumbled into many of the surrounding icy sculptures, crashing against each other like dominoes, causing their bodies to be smashed and scattered around the hall.

She made it to the hall entrance and ran across to the gardens. She slammed open the door without even noticing that the glass had been blown from its window. The sound scared the birds from the ground into the sky and surrounding trees. She ran over the broken glass that lay in the snow and it crunched into her shoes.

She stopped in her tracks. She was unable to escape the horrors Sylvie had caused around her. Dotted all around the grounds were bodies. Bodies of the children. The snow was splattered with red. Blood had flown from the children's bodies as they were thrown through the windows throughout the orphanage. As Sylvie once was, their bodies now lay in the cold, glittering snow with no one but Nora to grieve for them.

Having been inside baking whilst Mr Hughes got rid of Sylvie's body, she had no idea where her body had been buried. She knew she would have to bury these girls just as he had buried Sylvie. She couldn't just leave them in the snow for the crows to peck at.

Mr Hughes had left the wheelbarrow and shovel in the open from when he had buried Sylvie, but any tracks he had once made were filled with fresh snow. Looking at all the lifeless bodies in the snow left her feeling totally helpless. How was she to bury all of these bodies? The wheelbarrow was small, so only one body would fit each time.

She thought about informing the police, but there would be so many questions, and with her being the only person left alive, who's to say they wouldn't accuse her of murder? Burying them was her only option. With teary eyes, she picked up the handles of the wheelbarrow and pushed it towards the nearest body. She had to push hard to force it through the thickness, and when she reached the body, sobs burst from within her.

She had noticed the birds fleeing when she ran out the door, but she hadn't noticed they had already been feeding off the children's remains. The girl before her was missing an eye, leaving a gaping hole where her once blue sparkling eye had been, and there were gouges in her cheeks where they had torn at her flesh.

Although the birds had done their best to make her unidentifiable, Nora knew this child well. It had been Elizabeth. She had returned to the home minus any authority after sending her to fetch the police. Her body was a mess from the fall she had taken. Arms and legs twisted out of their joints and glass fragments had impaled themselves all over her small body.

She knelt in the snow and wept for the girl she had considered her own. Her warm tears dripped into the icy blanket, leaving melted little holes from their descent where they then turned to ice.

She wiped her eyes and pulled herself up, her hands gripping the rusted, rough wheelbarrow. She closed her eyes one more time before leaning down to pick up Elizabeth's lifeless body and placing her in the wheelbarrow. The torso was stiff and heavy, like a concrete statue in her arms. She struggled, and instead of placing her in gently, she dropped her, and her heavy frozen body made a loud bang as it collided with the metal tray. Again, a sob escaped Nora's mouth as the noise echoed in her ears. She would never forget that sound, never forget this scene or what she was about to do.

She wheeled her body against the deep snow, pushing as hard as she could as the thick substance pushed back. She came to a small clearing and started to dig. The ground was hard, making digging impossible. She noticed a pile a little distance over. It had looked like a mound from a badger digging his way out of the ground; something must have disturbed his winter slumber. She didn't care, she only knew it would be easier to dig where the ground had already been unsettled.

She stuck the shovel into the dirt and started shifting it. She didn't have to remove very much until she came across something. Sylvie's body. She lay there, non-decomposing, fully preserved by the cold ground around her.

"My Lord, please... Please help me." She cried when she realised what she had done. She held onto the chain around her neck whilst she prayed for her Lord to give her strength and caressed the symbol that dangled from it between her thumbs and fingers. An upside-down cross set inside a circle with what appeared to be twisted horns surrounding it. Finishing her dark prayer, she continued to dig into the ground to the side of Sylvie's body, where the ground was slightly easier to dig rather than moving elsewhere.

Having dug a hole big enough for the small girl in the barrow, she lifted the body and fell back down onto her knees before placing her into the ground next to Sylvie. She said a small prayer before she started to shift the soil back over their bodies, encasing them in the cold ground forever.

"I can't do this," she cried out, but her words were lost in the wind.

Through her sobs, she heard a train in the distance. The little woodland area only went on for a few meters before revealing a large field belonging to a local farmer, and on the other side of the field were the railway tracks. It had recently been installed, and over the past few weeks had been so popular they increased the frequency of trains, making it more accessible for people who worked both night and day.

The nearest station was about an hour's walk from the orphanage, but the tracks were only fifteen minutes away. As soon as she heard the train, she knew what her next steps would be.

One final tear dropped from her burning eyes and into the empty wheelbarrow before she turned and faced the field. She had made her mind up. She couldn't bear burying the rest of the children and staff; it was too much for her. The bodies of the children she had taught, not even thinking about how badly they were treated, just that she couldn't bury another body. She stumbled through the remaining section of trees before heading out into the barren field.

During the summer the crops had been bountiful, but now in the freezing winter, snow covered the many acres like a brand-new, unused, fluffy blanket. Nora started making her way through the several inches of snow, ruining the blank canvas it had been. It was so deep it reached her knees, soaking her clothes, and coldness seeped right through to her bones. She was numb. Inside and out. Tears had stopped falling and she was zombie-like in the way she moved. Emotionless, she dragged her body slowly through the snow, her face like stone as she left a long trail behind her.

She was near the rails when she heard the train nearing. Just a few more steps and she would be on the tracks. The snow had been cleared from them by the men working on them throughout the day. The sky was already dark as four thirty came around, and there were no lights to illuminate the tracks. The only light that eventually came was that of the oil lamp attached to the front of the steam engine headed her way. It was only a faint beam, but it indicated the train was nearing and she stepped onto the track. The lantern did not give the driver enough sight ahead to bring the engine to a stop before colliding with Nora's body.

She stood in front of it, her eyes frozen in her head. She remained unmoving and silent even when the four hundred and ninety-five tons of metal and steam collided with her and crushed every bone in her body as it sounded its loud horn.

CHAPTER
THIRTEEN
RIDDLE ME THIS

JENNY SIPPED HER SOUP. The contents were hot and steamy, the texture thick in her mouth. Tomato soup, and fresh she would guess. She hadn't had homemade soup in forever. She had been planning to take advantage of the summer holidays and start baking and trying out different recipes while her fiancé was at work. Apple pies, fruit tarts, all kinds of different soups that she could freeze and use in the autumn when hopefully she would find new employment, but of course, that plan went out the window as soon as she found him screwing that other woman on his desk.

The thought of their bodies pressed up against each other, their fingers caressing one another's skin, his tongue slipping inside of that whore's mouth and playing with her tongue.

She quickly shook her head to rid her brain of the awful imprint. Her focus went back to the soup on her lap. Now she would enjoy someone else's efforts of hearty soups rather than her own, and she would do so whilst she worked out what in hell's name was happening in this place.

The warm soup and the never-ending stormy weather outside were making her tired. There was something comforting about the storm. Its low rumbles, the pitter-pattering of the raindrops against her window, the flickers of flames on the small candles beside her, with a tray holding her soup and orange juice. Any onlookers would believe it to be the middle of autumn with how cosy the room appeared.

It was, ironically, a warm welcome to what had happened to her only moments ago. She was either going insanely crazy, or there were horrors worse than her worst nightmares happening in and around the school. As she gulped down her orange juice, in hopes to wake herself up a little, delicate taps echoed from the door.

"Miss Hart? You sent for me?" a small voice called from the other side. She had almost forgotten she asked for Abigail to come to her room.

"Yes, come in Abigail," Jenny answered before yawning. She had no idea how she would even approach Abigail about what she wanted to ask. Abigail was just a small girl, and she was probably already frightened by what had happened downstairs. Jenny would have to be gentle with how she approached her.

Abigail pushed the door open, a beam of light from her own candle flooding into the room as she stepped inside and closed the door behind her.

"Have I done something wrong, Miss?" she questioned, her little voice filled with anxiety.

"No, no. Of course you haven't, Abigail. What would make you think that? Come, sit on the end of the bed." Jenny patted the bed with her hand in a motion for her to sit with her.

"We're only usually called to staff quarters if we have done something wrong, Miss." She made her way slowly over to the bed and perched on its edge.

"Trust me, you haven't," she said reassuringly. "I've called you up here as I need your help."

Abigail's gaze fell to her lap. She had an inkling about what Jenny would be asking, and nerves filled her up like a balloon from just thinking about it and caused her to start biting at the cracks in her lips.

"What happened downstairs, it wasn't my imagination, was it? You gave me a look before I came up here," she said gently.

Abigail continued biting at her chapped lips and pulling at dried skin around her fingernails, making them bleed.

"Abigail, please, you can trust me," she begged. She reached out her hand and placed it on Abigail's back hoping to be of some comfort.

"I'll get in trouble, Miss. The other girls and Miss May will have my guts for garters, Miss. We vowed never to mention anything. The walls have ears, Miss. I cannot."

Jenny looked at Abigail and then around the room, her eyes investigating every crevice, every nook and cranny, every crease for signs of motion or gaps through which people could listen. She found none.

"I shouldn't have looked at you. I should have kept my head down. If anyone finds out that you even have a feeling that things weren't right and that I had something to do with that then they…"

"Will have your guts for garters?" Jenny interrupted, finishing Abigail's sentence.

"Yes, Miss."

"Well then, we can't have that, can we?" Jenny smiled at her.

Abigail looked up from her lap and into Jenny's eyes. They were soft and understanding. She wanted more than anything to help Jenny, but she couldn't tell her their secret. It had been kept for many, many years and if it were to be told now, she would ruin everything. Maybe she could try to hint at something that wouldn't lead her directly to the truth, but let her know that this wasn't any ordinary place.

"The library has books that can lead to as many doors as the imagination can handle; your only task is finding the right door."

Jenny looked at her puzzled.

"Find the door to find the truth," she whispered before looking back down at her hands. Her fingers were trembling and her palms were sweating. Jenny could see that whatever she had just told her was important but dangerous.

"I must go, Miss. My peers will wonder what is taking me so long," she said in a hushed voice.

"Good luck with your reading, Miss Hart," she said loud enough for anyone who may be listening. "There are some great books for your imagination in the library, lots of puzzles and mysteries." She grabbed her candle from the chest of drawers and made her way out the door. "Good night, Miss Hart."

"Good night, Abigail," Jenny replied, but a little too late. Abigail had already closed the door behind her, leaving just half the amount of light in the room.

Jenny thought about what Abigail had said. *Did she just give me a riddle? Doors, books, the library, imagination. 'Find the door to find the truth' she had said. Do I need to find a book to find the door? There are hundreds of books in the library, where would I even begin? And what did she mean 'The walls have ears?'*

She looked around the room once more and a thought struck her. Thinking back, Jenny remembered her first evening at the school and how she came to find Lenora standing behind her out of nowhere. She hadn't worked out how she had managed to get there so silently without her noticing, but Abigail saying the walls have ears made her question whether there was actually a secret doorway. *Was this the secret Abigail was talking about? It would partly make sense. It would explain how Lenora got into the room while she was sleeping and placed the clothes at the end of her bed.*

But the room was small. It just about fit a bed, the bedside table, a chest of drawers, and a wardrobe next to the fireplace. There was a door next to the fireplace which led to her en-suite, but again that wasn't very luxurious. It was more of a shower room and could definitely do with a makeover. It looked as though it hadn't been touched since the late 1800s, with only an old shower that looked like a cage. It made her hairs stand up on end. It didn't feel right in there. It could be that the room was only just big enough for the shower to be installed. It was basically a large cupboard. There was no way there was a secret door to be found in her room.

The library was her next clue. Abigail had said find the books that lead to doors. With what had happened in the hall, Jenny had a feeling that if she were to wander about, her actions would definitely be watched, and the way Abigail had talked about Miss May and the other children, she had no idea who would be spying on her. She would have to be careful about her next plan of action. If she were to get caught, who knows what would happen to her or to Abigail if it was found she had been the one to lead Jenny down this path.

Sitting in her bed, sipping her soup and thinking about what to do, she felt as though the walls were watching her, waiting for her to make her decision. A pulse in her head was drumming against her skull. She dropped her spoon into the half-empty bowl, splattering liquid tomato droplets over herself and the white bed sheets.

Her vision started to swim and caused her confusion. A man stood at the end of her bed. From what she could make out between the swirls of colours flooding her eyes, he was a tall man in a black suit. The swimming blurs of coloured ink made it hard to notice any of the man's features.

"Please, help me?" Jenny begged as her head swayed like a boat on a stormy ocean. She received no reply from the strange man, but he made his way around the bed. One step after the other, thumping across the floorboards, closing in on her in multi-coloured ripples, every step he made sending another colour flooding away from him like rolling waves hitting the shore. Each wave flowing away from him caused Jenny to become more and more nauseated.

Her eyes left the man for a small second and focused on her soup on the lap tray. The contents swirled round and round like a whirlpool in the half-empty bowl. Her hand dropped onto one side of the tray, causing the bowl to fling from where it had sat. It went spinning *through* the man and smashed into the wall behind him. A deep, orange splatter dribbled down the white wall and onto the scruffy skirting boards.

The man was standing right next to her bed and started to pull the sheets off her. Jenny's limbs were heavy, and her body had lost all its strength. The only part of her still able to move was her eyes. Her dead-weight body lay there, unable to get away from the man before her. He leant in closer to her as he grabbed the top of the sheet. As he did, she was finally able make out his face.

"Hughes." The only word she was able to mumble out from her unmoving lips.

It was Mr Hughes. His receding hairline, his peppered moustache, his dark haunting eyes. He stepped backward, sheets in hand, revealing her wearing just a white, long nightgown. The room fell cold, and as if a gust of wind had blown through the room, the once warm fire was extinguished. Goose pimples appeared all over her body as the cold sank into her skin. She could feel the elements against her but was restrained from any motions against them. She was unable to pull the sheets back up to cover her cooling skin, unable to jump out of bed and restart the fire, unable to protect herself.

WUH-TSHH!

A braided whip snapped against her bare legs, the cold now no longer her main enemy, as hot red gashes appeared on her skin. Blood seeped and ran down her legs onto the sheets. The warm liquid seeped into the cotton fibres and left puddles of red blotches.

She wanted more than anything to scream and pull her legs close to her body to comfort herself, but she couldn't. Instead, her scream was trapped in her throat as though someone's hands had tightened around her neck. The only noise she could make was a dull breath that tried to escape her, begging to escape her throat and out of her lips.

WUH-TSHH!

Another blow hit just above the previous wounds. It wasn't long until Jenny was lying in a pool of her own blood. Not being able to withstand any more pain from the lashing Mr Hughes was bringing down on her, her vision faded out, and just before she was gone to the darkness, a horrific, evil laugh bellowed in her ears.

CHAPTER FOURTEEN
THE OTHER LIBRARY

HER SCREAM INFESTED THE DARKNESS like a plague; it spread into every crevice of her unconscious mind. In the darkness of her subconscious, she stood alone, a black shadow spreading from her feet all around her, reaching all spaces but one.

A dark tunnel lay ahead of her, tiny fragments of light glittering along its walls, exposing rough, dark bricks and drawing her into its depths. The heinous laugh that had invaded her ears seemed to echo back at her, bouncing off the tunnel walls. Taunting her. Making her quiver in fear as the horrid voice encircled her.

She ran through the tunnel in an attempt to free herself from the monstrous voice. The sounds of her feet attacking the ground as she ran made it sound as though there were many more than only her two feet pounding the ground. She looked back as she carried on, pushing herself forward. A face followed after her, gaining on her. *HIS* face! The face matched the evil, growling cackle that chased her.

Jenny's foot collided with something on the ground. She fell face-first into a massive pile of books. Looking up, the tunnel and the face of Mr Hughes had all but vanished. She was in a library. Awake and with cuts and bruises all over her legs. The wounds from the lashings had been real and were smeared with dried blood that threatened to reopen at the slightest touch. Some were still weeping as the muscles in her legs had caused her skin to tighten from her run.

She was right in the middle of a mountain of thousands of books. She couldn't work out how she had got here when she was last awake in her bed. One possible explanation was sleepwalking. She had heard that stress could cause a ton of sleep disturbances, including sleepwalking. *That must be it. It has to be.*

She pulled herself up, causing more books to tumble around her. Paperbacks and hardbacks attacked each other as they dropped to the floor. This wasn't the library she knew of, the one she had previously looked through books to read, the one she had sent the students to. This one was bigger and smelt musty.

The only light that filled the room was that of the lightning that continued to flash relentlessly. Each flash highlighted the room, so she saw only glimpses of what was around her. Large bookshelves lined the walls and were full of old, dusty books, and half-melted-down candles sat on almost every surface. She climbed out from the heap of damaged books, sending a cloud of dust into the air as she clambered her way over to the shelves.

She trod over stacks of novels and newspapers, trying not to stumble in the darkness. Her eyes wouldn't adjust to her surroundings and so the next flash of lightning came a little too late. She walked straight into what she could only assume was a desk. Her upper half bent over it as she collided with the hefty wooden furniture.

She hoped she would be able to find a lamp of some kind. Her hands fumbled over the desk. There were more books, papers, and large feathers that she could only imagine were used as quills, a machine she believed to be an old typewriter the way the little buttons felt under her fingertips, and then a small box that felt rough along the edge. Matches!

It wasn't a lamp, but it would sure help. All she needed to do now was reach the candles on the copious amount of shelves without bumping into something else. If she hurled over something else the way she did the desk, she knew she would drop the matches, and they would be a nightmare to find amongst the papers and books that were scattered around the floor.

Hands out in front of her, one hand tightly around the small, card box, she took slow steps, dragging her feet along the ground so she could feel her way using her feet and not trip over anything unexpectedly. Carefully, she made her way through the minefield of books, reached the bookcase, and grabbed the first candle her hand stumbled upon. She placed it directly in front of her and struck a match against the side of the box. No flame. It sparked a little but didn't ignite. She tried a second time, and as she did the flame lit up the room and a face appeared only inches away from hers! The flame's glow focused on the evil eyes that stared at her menacingly.

Her shock caused the flame to blow out as she stumbled backward over a pile of books stacked behind her. The matches luckily fell beside her, and she quickly thumbed to strike another match. The face and the person it belonged to had gone. She knew it was the face of Mr Hughes. She'd seen his face too many times now for it not to be recognisable. But what did he want with her? Was he just out to get everyone regardless of their age?

She was no little schoolgirl who quivered in the face of a violent man, but this man was a dead one. He wasn't somebody she could fight against or have the police lock up.

The more he revealed himself, the more she thought she was on the right track. It was as though he was trying to scare her away from finding the truth behind Old Eden School. Jenny was more stubborn than many believed her to be. Her innocent exterior masked her strength and determination. No one was going to stop her now. Not Lenora, and certainly not some dead, abusive psychopath.

Jenny was starting to become angry with the man. What he did to those girls, the way he was trying to frighten her. Enough was enough. The flame had already burnt down halfway and was starting to warm her fingertips. She huffed and stood, the match held high in the air to avoid it burning anything around her. She quickly wafted the match around in the air to put the flame out as it reached her fingers. The heat pricked them as a warning that if left, the flame would burn her.

There was only one match left as she pulled the little tray from its cardboard box. She couldn't mess this up. If she did, she would be stuck in the library until dawn broke. Without proper light, she was blind to her exit. She struck the final match against the rough edge and it ignited. This time no face, no strange thing lurking in the dark. She tipped the candle in front of her and lit it before lighting another on the shelf above.

Having two candles lit, she could now see what was immediately in front of her. She continued to light the rest of the candles around the room with the first candle. The room was filled with glowing light, showing every book, every sheet of paper, and every knick-knack in the room.

The library was painted black, and its bookcases matched its malevolent backdrop. The only thing she couldn't see was a way out. *How the hell did I even get in here?* she questioned herself. The last she knew, she was in a daze in her own bed. Now she stood in a library that was not the library she knew of, and there seemed to be no way in or out of the room. *I must have got in here somehow. I couldn't just appear in random places throughout the school now, could I?*

Could I?

Jenny started to feel as if she was actually going insane. All the madness that happened in the hall, her seemingly passing out in her bedroom, waking up in what appeared to be a tunnel, then somehow falling into this library. It was all complete madness.

"Come on, Jenny. Wake up." She slapped herself hard around the face, the impact making her cheek sting. After wincing from the smack she gave herself, she opened her eyes. She was still there, in the library, trapped.

Her heart sped up and her throat dried out. She kept trying to wet her mouth with her tongue and swallow, but it was like swallowing sand. She felt the need to cough, but her windpipe started to squeeze shut. That, along with the sweat that had formed across her forehead, indicated that the anxiety of being stuck in this room had started to get to her. She didn't normally suffer from claustrophobia, but with everything that had happened to her in the past few days, this was the cherry on top of the fucked up cake.

Jenny's body became heavy, her legs trembling as the idea of being stuck in this God-forsaken building crept into every pore of her body. *No, come on. You can't let this get the better of you. Focus on what you need to do. You need to figure out the riddle. What was Abigail trying to tell you?*

She closed her eyes, took a deep breath, and opened them after the shaky breath was released. She looked around the room for any clues as she continued with her deep breaths, anything that would coincide with what Abigail had told her.

The books. Soft candlelight glowed enough for Jenny to start rummaging through the books on the shelves. These weren't any old, ordinary books. She scanned the titles. *Honouring the Devil. Communicating with Evil. I sold My Soul. Black Spells. The Dark Church. Blood Magick.* Book upon book focused on evil. What the hell had been going on here? She knew Victorians were into the macabre, but this was on a whole other level. A whole library dedicated to the macabre and, apparently, the Devil.

She soon realised it wasn't just the books that suggested someone was meddling with things they shouldn't be. Not only did the books give it away, but the other items lined the bookshelves and walls. Chains holding shackles hung from the wall, and branding irons sat by the sooty fireplace. Several jars were filled with yellowish fluids, but it was the items in the fluids! Severed hands, toes, and... nipples? *No, surely not?* She lifted the candle up closer to the jar with floating discs. She gasped and covered her mouth, focusing on not throwing up her guts. The other items seemed mundane compared to the jars. There was a collection of different sized skulls dotting the room.

By the fireplace stood some metal tools, At first, she believed the irons to be cleaning tools for the fireplace, but upon closer inspection, they were tools for branding. One branded end showed the letters TH. As soon as she saw them, she knew instantly that they were the initials of Tobias Hughes. What the hell was he using these for? Jenny could imagine, but the thought was so dark and unpleasant she didn't want it in her mind. The other tool was a symbol. It was round, but she couldn't clearly make out what the other parts were.

She placed the branding irons back by the fireplace and headed back over to the books, still being careful not to trip over the ones that were thrown all over the floor, their pages showing images of sacrifice, torture, and weird symbols. She tried to ignore the images and just focus on the books on the shelves. She pulled one after the other from the dusty unit, flicking through yellowed pages dotted with mould. None of the contents screamed anything to her that would indicate anything Abigail had hinted at. *Come on, give me a sign, please!* And just as the thought escaped her, a black book fell from the shelf on the other side of the room, onto the dusty carpet. She climbed over the mess on the floor and grabbed the book.

It had definitely seen better days. It was a hardback, covered in a dark material that had started fraying at the edges, revealing the brown material beneath it. On the cover, the words *Curses and Hexes of our Dark Lord* were displayed in a silver cursive embroidery that had some kind of splatter across it. The colour muddied the silver-threaded words, and all Jenny could think was that it was blood.

She opened the book up and the first page had an inscription. *Page 104 - To trap a soul. Thank me later. Dad.* Below the message was another symbol. It had markings similar to that of the branding iron. It was a circle with two twisted horns and an upside-down cross in its center.

Mr Hughes' dad? she thought to herself. She couldn't fathom who else this would have belonged to. The branding irons indicated they belonged to Tobias Hughes, so surely the other items in there, including the tatty old book, also belonged to him.

She flicked through the crispy pages, the edges splattered with dried, old blood that held some of the pages together. She found page 104. It depicted images of what appeared to be people trapped behind bars, helpless souls reaching out as if asking the reader to release them.

She imagined Tobias holding the book in his hands, an evil glare in his eye as he read the words on the pages out loud and used it against anyone who crossed him. *What if he used this against the girls?* she wondered fearfully.

She placed the book on the desk and was about to take a seat when she heard a shuffling noise behind her. The book had knocked over the inkwell, which had been a lever in disguise. The bookcase behind her had opened up, pushing the books on the floor into another pile and out of the way. It revealed a staircase lit by a flaming torch. She couldn't work out how it was alight; someone surely must have had to light it with a match or a lighter.

She picked up the book from the messy desk, luckily the spilt ink hadn't touched it, and drifted slowly inside the once-concealed entrance. Sticky spider webs hung in wispy threads, a cool air caused them to sway above her head. Heading up a few of the concrete steps, she noticed just how dark the rest of the stairway was. There were no more torches lining the way, so she stepped back down and fetched the torch from the wall at the bottom of the stairs.

The climb was steep as she held onto the rope along the wall for stability between breaths. The steps seemed to keep going and going, without revealing where they lead. Just as she was about to stop again to rest her wobbly legs, she noticed a door ahead of her, just four more steps away. Encouraging her legs to keep moving, she climbed the last few steps and twisted the door handle. It was stiff, but as she leant inwards it clicked open. She recognised the room before her instantly. It was her own.

The doorway had been hidden behind her wardrobe all along. She would never have thought to move a wardrobe to find a secret door. This had been strategic. Whoever had done this did so on purpose. They had done this to hide the library full of evil objects. She knew there and then that the room she was staying in was definitely Tobias's room, no ifs or buts. This was his room and his secret library. This man wasn't just a horrid one, he was an evil one. He dealt with the devil and if not the devil, then demons. Whatever it was, it wasn't good. Then it occurred to her. Was it really Tobias Hughes that had been evil? Or had he been led down a path that caused him to be taken over? To be possessed by whatever evil he had been dealing with.

She looked back down at the ratty book still in her hands. It had been given to him by his father. Had this been a family thing? Perhaps a cult even? So many thoughts and ideas swam around her brain.

CHAPTER
FIFTEEN
SUSPICIONS

JENNY PLACED THE TORCH in the metal holder on the inside of the hidden stairway before pushing the wardrobe door back into the wall. It was heavy to push and dragged across the floor until it was fully flush against the wall, and a clicking noise confirmed the entrance was secured.

Her room was back in darkness now that the staircase was hidden. She had placed the book on the windowsill before closing the entrance. With her hand on the wall, she fumbled across to the window. The storm seemed to be slowing, the lightning having died down, and it no longer lit up the glass. She stepped blindly across the room. Having reached the window, the rain still being forced against its glass leaving watery trails behind its drops, her fingertips felt along the cold, damp windowsill until they found the thick book she had placed there. She picked it up and placed it under her arm so her hands were still free to help her find her way away through the room.

She held her hands out in front of her, trying to make her way back to her bed, when she stepped onto the broken shards of the bowl she'd forgotten had gone flying from her lap earlier on. She collapsed to the floor with a loud thud, a sharp piece of soup-encrusted pottery wedged into the arch of her foot. The book slid from her hands and across the floor, under the bed, and onto the other side of the room by the door.

Screaming out in pain, she clutched her foot tightly in her hands, putting tight pressure on the skin surrounding her bloody wound. The pain soaring through her foot was so intense her vision went blurry, causing a sheet of blackness to appear across her eyes and tiny little sparkles to flicker in the darkness.

She opened her eyes, but darkness still surrounded her. She could barely see the outline of the shard in her foot, but she could definitely feel where it was. She pinched the fragment between her thumb and fingers, reluctant to pull. It took a few moments for her to build up the courage to pull it out. *Three, two, one...* Her eyelids squeezed together, and she ripped the piece of bowl from her foot. Blood squirted from the wound and seeped into the floorboards, creating a pool of warm blood.

Jenny pressed her hand tightly against the open cut and with her other hand felt the air around her in hopes she was near her bed. No luck. Her hand glided through nothing but space. She released her foot and crawled on all fours until she brushed up against the side of her bed. Stopping next to it and changing position, she pulled the sheet from the bed and ripped at the corner. The cotton frayed as she tore a strip from it. She wrapped the cloth around her foot, pulling it tightly as she wrapped it around the wound.

Blood seeped through the fabric, but the layers slowed the bleed. Only a small amount of spotting was visible on the outside of the makeshift bandage.

A creaking noise sounded on the other side of the room and a small glow came inside. Jenny sat still on the floor, not making a sound. Small, soft footsteps trod inside the door, across the floorboards, and towards the bed, and the light became brighter as it grew nearer.

"Jenny?" Lenora questioned, noticing the bed a mess, the fragments of bowl around the floor, the soup stains up the wall and splatters on the bed. Lenora held a candle over the bed, just far enough over to see Jenny on the floor, knees pulled in tight to her chest and blood covering her legs. She rushed round to the other side of the bed to where Jenny was sitting. Her eyes fell on the small puddle of blood and the streak that had been created where she had dragged her bloody foot behind her.

"Jenny, what in the hell happened?" she asked as she continued examining the room. She saw the scratches on the floor from where the wardrobe had been pushed open and closed, leaving a sort of circular marking on the floorboards. She tried to pretend she didn't see it and instead focused solely on Jenny and the blood.

She placed her candle on the set of drawers and helped Jenny onto the bed. Jenny held onto her arms and winced as she tried to put her weight on her foot. Jenny stayed silent, not entirely sure what to tell her. She knew for a fact she couldn't trust her. She was hiding so much, but Jenny was unaware of how much and what she had been lying about. Sitting on the bed, she stared at her bandaged foot, avoiding eye contact with Lenora.

Lenora took her candle and relit Jenny's that was sitting on the bedside table. The room could be seen a lot clearer now. Placing her own candle back on the chest of drawers, she walked into the shower room and grabbed some of the towels hanging on the back of the door. Walking back into the bedroom, her gaze was fixed on Jenny. *What is she doing awake? She should be passed out with the dose I gave her. What the blazes has she been doing?* Lenora placed a towel over the blood on the floor to soak up the red puddle.

Jenny could feel Lenora's eyes fixated on her, but she refrained from meeting her gaze. Her heart raced inside her chest as she tried to think of what to say. If she mentioned feeling weird and that Mr Hughes had visited her, Lenora would either think Jenny to be crazy; or Lenora knew the school was haunted and hid it from her. Why would she not just come forward and tell her about any ghosts that may be roaming the halls? At least then she would know she wasn't going nuts. She would be more prepared for what to look out for and could make sure the children were safe. She couldn't know, surely not. She couldn't come to a good enough conclusion as to why Lenora would keep that from her. It didn't make sense.

"I fell asleep when I was eating the soup and ended up having a nightmare. I must have freaked out and sent my bowl flying. I went to clean it up and stood on a shard." That was the best she could come up with without letting on that she knew something else was going on in the school. She only hoped that Lenora believed her enough to not question her.

"That's my fault. I shouldn't have left before taking your tray. I should have stayed with you whilst you ate."

"No, Lenora," she started, worrying that Lenora would never leave her side. "You're not my mum or nurse. I'm not your responsibility. I should have been more careful."

"Well, that's neither here nor there. You're a member of my staff and obviously not well. I should have made sure you were okay before leaving you to rest. How is your foot? Do you need something to ease the pain?"

"Please? I think it will be fine, but some tablets to help with the pain would be nice."

"Okay, I'll come back up with something. Then you must rest. The children are now all in their beds for the night. Hopefully, this storm will have passed by the morning so we can start functioning as normal." Lenora walked towards the door, grabbing her candle on the way. "I'll be back in a moment." As she reached the door, she noticed the book laying on the floor up against the wall. The silver embroidery shone under her candlelight. She quickly shifted her eyes from the book and back to the door.

Lenora shut the door behind her as she stepped out into the hallway. There, waiting for her next to the door, was Lizzie.

"What can I do to help, Miss?" she whispered.

"Keep an eye on her. She should have been passed out from the soup. The mushrooms in it would have given her hallucinations and the laudanum should have caused her to pass out. Instead, she is awake and seems to have destroyed her room.

She also has one of Mr Hughes' books. I don't know how she found it. There were scratch marks on the floor. Someone's been in the Dark Library."

"It couldn't have been her, surely? How would she know about it? No one would have told her."

"I don't know. That's why I need you to keep an eye on her. Make sure she doesn't go on walkabouts in the night. Leave the rest to me. We need to come up with a plan before she finds out why she's really here. The only way I want her to find out is when it's too late."

"Agreed," Lizzie nodded and turned to the cupboard next to Jenny's room. To anyone else, it would look like a normal airing cupboard to store spare towels and sheets, but Lizzie knew differently. She climbed underneath the several shelves lined with fluffy towels and fresh sheets and pushed on the back of the cupboard. A false wall.

The fake backing led to a passage behind Jenny's bedroom. Abigail wasn't wrong when she said the walls have eyes. Jenny didn't notice earlier as she was sitting on the bed looking outward. She didn't know that above the bed was a small gap in the wooden slats lining the wall above the bed frame. Lizzie looked through the thin gap, just big enough to be able to see through so that anyone on the other side wouldn't be able to see their spying eyes.

The room was still and lit by the soft glow of the unflickering candle that sat next to Jenny's bed. She could see just the top of Jenny's head as she sat on the mattress, talking to herself.

"What should I do?" Jenny questioned. She sat in silence, her hand holding onto her foot as she started to feel strange again. The only thing she could think of was that it must be related to the soup. She had sipped from the bowl before the first episode had started, and this time, the china fragment that had impaled her foot had dried soup remnants crusted around its edges.

The room swayed around her as she flopped backward on the bed. Eyes closed or open, it didn't matter. The world still felt as though it was circling around her. The motion caused her to feel as though she was on a swaying ship, her head flowing about as if her body was floating on waves.

Suddenly the room stopped swaying and faded into a scene on the ocean. Her body appeared to be on a raft, logs tied together, waves thrashing at its sides, and the storm around her building back up and sending flashes of lightning striking at the ferocious sea.

Lizzie, still spying on her from the airing cupboard, could see Jenny thrashing about on the bed as if having the most intense nightmare.

"Has to be the laudanum," she whispered to herself, watching as Jenny's body twisted and turned, her fingers scratching at her body. She could only think that the laudanum had a delayed reaction and the hallucinations had finally started to kick in.

What she didn't know was someone was in her drug induced dream, helping her through them.

"Jenny," a voice whispered over the thrashing waves of her mind. She looked around the stormy sea and saw a girl in the distance standing on top of the angry waters.

"Jenny, calm your mind. Slow your breathing. This is all in your head. You need to wake up. There are things you need to know. Old Eden is not as it appears to be. You need to find the answers."

"What do you mean?" she asked as she tried to steady herself on the rickety raft.

"The book," the voice was drifting away from her.

"What book?"

"The Dark Lord's book." The small image floated out of sight.

"Wait! Why me? Why is this happening?" But the little girl had been lost to the waves.

She remembered what the girl had instructed her to do. Calm her mind. Slow her breathing. She focused on her breath, slowing it down to bring it to a steadier pace that relieved the burning inside her throat. As her breathing became more balanced, the waves calmed around her, and the storm, once angry and abusive, was silenced. She lay back on the lightly swaying raft and placed her hands flat against the wet wood. She softly closed her eyes.

"Wake up," she whispered to herself.

When she opened her eyes, she was back in her bed. The room was still a soupy, bloody mess from the previous events. She lay there for a moment, appreciating being warm and dry and no longer swaying in a stormy ocean. The girl's words played over in her head as she rested. *The Dark Lord's Book.* Her head tipped to one side, facing the wall, and her eyes fell upon the book she had brought up from the secret library. *Curses and Hexes of our Dark Lord.* The letters shone in the candlelight.

She slowly pulled herself up in bed so she was sitting upright, her head resting back on the headboard. The room around her spun for a moment as black and silver dots invaded her vision, still not one hundred percent over being unknowingly drugged. As soon as her head stopped spinning and the dots had vanished from her eyes, she reached over to the book on the floor, one hand holding her weight while the rest of her body stayed on the bed. Her other hand grabbed hold of the black book and she clumsily, one-handed, pushed herself back upright on her bed.

She let her head steady again as the book rested on top of the crinkled, soup-splattered bed sheets. The black and white dots left her vision, and she slowly opened her eyes to let them fall on the book in her lap.

"What is it you're keeping secret?" she whispered to it as her fingers ran across the leather-bound cover.

She gently opened the book, anxious about what she would find. Of course, she had already read the inscription inside the cover, but she sensed that what she was about to read would be dark and dangerous, and she wasn't wrong. Flipping slowly from page to page, she read what seemed to be prayers, devotions, correspondences, and spells of an evil nature. How to invoke demons to torture your enemies, how to get them to obey your every will. She came across a bookmark, an old black and white photo of a child.

The image showed a young girl, one that she recognised, and from the name written below the photo her suspicions were confirmed. Abigail. The young girl from her class. But how? This photo was so old, it couldn't be her, could it? She had been acting as if she knew something and had wanted to help Jenny work it out.

"She can't be dead! Can she?" Jenny sat in confusion and placed the photo beside her to see what page Abigail had been saving for the last person who used the book.

The title across the top of the page was written in Latin, and although she never studied the dead language, there was no denying that she understood what it read. Familia Sacrificium. Underneath it read: To sacrifice one's family, to free oneself. The passage below described how to get the dead to obey your every order, and that if a soul (your soul) was trapped in the unknown, then by sacrificing your last remaining kin, your soul would be free as theirs would take your place.

"Abigail was his descendant?" She was in shock. She couldn't understand how anyone could be so evil and yet have a descendant like Abigail, whose innocence shone brightly from within. She was also still unaware of the eyes that remained watching her every move from right behind her.

Lizzie had just witnessed what Jenny discovered and crawled silently out of the hidden cupboard where she had been spying from. She crept down the hall and into the library where Miss May was working. She pushed the library door open to find her sitting at the desk, rain hitting hard against the glass panes lit by glowing candlelight.

"Miss, she's working it out! She has the Dark Lord's book. She knows about Abigail. It's only a matter of time until she works out the rest!"

"That damned book. I saw it on my way out of her room, sitting right by the door, but I couldn't grab it without her seeing and asking loads of questions. I was hoping she would just go to sleep and forget about the book. Damn her to hell." She bashed her fist against the wooden desk so hard the candle flames almost flickered out. She stood abruptly, her chair crashing to the ground.

"She will most definitely find out, and when she does, it will be too late."

CHAPTER SIXTEEN FAMILIA SACRIFICIUM

JENNY CONTINUED FLICKING THROUGH the book, spell after spell, potion after weird potion. One of the pages caught her eye. This one appeared to be a handwritten diary entry from Tobias himself. But it wasn't what she expected at all. This was an entry after death.

I have failed. Abigail wasn't the final heir. This can only mean one thing. The night I laid with that woman of the night, Joselyne. I know I was being careless, she must have had a child, my child. I must find out who my last living kin is to be able to break free.

The Dark Lord has provided me with the spells and secrets to make the other trapped spirits do my bidding and lead the heir to me, but he will not help any further. It is down to me to break free.

I cannot be stuck here with all these children and that damned woman. Lenora is so obsessed with me that I have to hide in the shadows. In life, I thought I could eventually be rid of her, but now that we are all stuck here, I am doomed unless I can find my kin and perform the Familia Sacrificium. For now, I will have to use the obsessive bitch to bring the heir to me, and once I've performed the sacrifice, I shall be free of her and these blasted brats. Damn them. Damn Sylvie. Damn Abigail. And damn this blasted hell hole.

Jenny turned the page to find more entries and the last caught her attention most.

Lenora has finally found her. The last heir. My freedom is finally within my grasp. She is on her way and so is my reward.

"Who was on their way?" she asked out loud.

"Why you were," Nora replied. She had been standing in the dark doorway, completely unnoticed by Jenny because she was so engrossed in the book.

Nora lunged at her through the darkness. Jenny was startled, and almost didn't move in time. She was halfway off the bed when Nora's nails dug deep into the flesh of her exposed legs. Blood seeped from the jagged gouges on her thighs and calves, pooling around Nora's nails and dripping onto the bed, as Jenny wriggled and kicked to get away from the wretched woman.

"You won't get away from me, Jenny. I may be dead, but I can still hurt you just as much as if I were alive." She continued tearing at Jenny's legs as she thrashed around on the bed, leaving scratches and open wounds oozing with blood. Lizzie ran in from behind Nora, a glimmer of something big and shiny in her hands. Jenny felt an immense impact hit her hard in the back of her head, and the bedroom fell into darkness as she lost consciousness.

"Lizzie! She better still be alive!"

Lizzie dropped the spade that she had retrieved from the garden shed. Water splatters were left on the floor from where it had dripped whilst she ran with it. She bent down to where Jenny's body lay on the floor, covered in burgundy splatters that shimmered in the candlelight. She placed her ear over Jenny's mouth and heard her shallow breaths.

"She's breathing," Lizzie confirmed. As she looked up at Nora, she noticed the rest of the girls standing by the doorway. They had all heard the commotion and had watched from the hallway.

"Does this mean Mr Hughes will converse with the Dark Lord for our freedom?" one of the girls asked.

Nora sighed with a small smile on her face. "It does. We just need to get her down to Mr Hughes."

Abigail was standing in the group of girls, fear plastered across her face. She knew what Jenny would now have to face, as she had been there before in her very place. She stood there wishing there was something she could do. She thought back to the day she was led to her own death. Tobias had used his spells to force Sylvie to kill her. She was placed in a trance-like state and walked off the edge of a beam that had once struck out from the building. It was only after she plummeted to her death that she had come to realise she was being sacrificed.

As Abigail was taking step after step along the wooden beam, Tobias was standing below, in the shadows of the night, reciting from the Dark One's book. He was the one who put her in the trance, not Sylvie. He had just forced Sylvie to lead her to the beam. Sylvie had no control over her own actions, she was being used as a puppet. Every blink, every step, every word, a manipulation of Tobias's doing. Yes, it was Sylvie that had cursed him, but now, on the other side, he was more powerful than she ever thought he could be. She wanted no part in killing his heirs. She wanted them to live so his soul would be forever trapped. She just didn't realise he would be trapped with her.

When Abigail's body crashed to the ground, her limbs twisted and mangled, Tobias waited and waited. Nothing happened. The night remained still with only the stars above him making any movement.

Anger bubbled up inside of him. Why was the Dark Lord not fulfilling his promise? Whilst alive, Tobias always prayed to him, worshipped him, sacrificed for him, hell, even started the church of the Dark Lord and took the children from the orphanage to praise him too. He would do anything the Dark Lord asked of him and never asked for anything back. That was until his own death fell on him. He went to the Dark Lord and asked for mercy, asked to be freed from this children-filled tomb. After all of this and doing exactly as he was told to do, why hadn't he moved on? Why was he still stuck at the orphanage, surrounded by those blasted children?

"Why are we still here, Tobias?" Lenora asked. "Did we do something wrong? Did we not follow the Dark Lord's instructions."

"I did. You better have brought me the correct things, or so help me Dark Lord, I will make the rest of your unliving existence unbearable."

Lenora was shocked by how he had spoken to her. She had done everything she could for him and was loyal to him no matter what. She had taken strands of the girl's hair from her hairbrush, gathered saliva from the sink after she had brushed her teeth, and even collected a snotty rag from when she had a cold. All the items Tobias had needed to go through with the spell. So why hadn't it worked?

Tobias stalked his way back into the orphanage, school at that time, secluding himself from the children and Lenora. He paced in the library, trying to wrack his brains as to why the Dark Lord was not going through with his end of the deal. Then it struck him that Abigail may not have been the last of his kin. He opened the Dark Lord's book and started to write inside it how he believed there may still be kin of his out in the world due to a night of lust with a prostitute.

Abigail found herself waking up in the basement, no longer with her body, but in the dark depths of the building. When she found her way back to the main hall, the staff and children were all either frightened or crying, but at the back of the hall in the shadows, she saw Sylvie. A man was standing behind her with his hand resting firmly on her shoulder.

"I'm so sorry," Sylvie whimpered as small droplets fell from her dead eyes. Abigail started to approach them, but before she could take another step, they vanished. She was dead and alone and things really didn't improve from there. The other spirits still stuck in the orphanage hated her because she wasn't the key to their freedom. They didn't care that it wasn't her fault, just that they were still stuck there and she hadn't helped them to move on. There was nothing she could do about that though, and as a result, she had existed for years since her death and was bullied and neglected in her afterlife as much as she was in her former life.

Now it was Jenny's turn, but Abigail would have no part in it, not as long as she could help it. She had done what she could for Jenny without being caught by the others; now it was time to take it up a notch.

"Grab her arms, Lizzie. We need to get her down to the basement before she wakes up."

Lizzie wrapped her hands around Jenny's wrists while Nora took hold of her ankles, and after a count of three, they both lifted Jenny's unconscious body. In her unaware state, her weight had almost tripled, making Lizzie and Nora's job of getting her out of the room and down the stairs nearly impossible. Once they got to the door, Lizzie's arms gave way and Jenny's body hit the ground with an almighty thud.

"You stupid girl. You know if we mess this up then Mr Hughes will make sure the Dark Lord will keep you burning in your own special hell. Now pick her up, and this time don't drop her."

Lizzie didn't say a word. She wasn't scared of Nora, but she was scared of Tobias and the connection he had with the Dark Lord himself. No one even knew his name, only Tobias was allowed to know that. If anyone else knew, they would also be able to talk with him and ask him about things. This way Tobias was able to keep the connection for himself and no one could get in the way of his plan.

They managed to get Jenny's body down the stairs and to the basement door under the stairs.

"You! Go into my left pocket, get the key, and open this damn door, will you?" she spat at one of the girls nearby. The girl placed the key in its lock and twisted it until it clicked into place and the door opened slightly, leaving a tiny gap. Nora shoved the girl out of the way with her large behind and continued to carry Jenny inside.

The rest of the girls followed behind, taking slow steps down into the darkness. They shifted past the old furniture and boxes of school work to the back of the basement. They came to a stop by an old, dusty wardrobe and placed Jenny on the floor. With Lizzie on one side of the cupboard and Nora the other, they pushed the wardrobe to one side, its heavy stature dragging across the concrete ground, screeching loudly as it was hauled and left a dust-free patch in front of a once concealed entrance.

Taking the ring of keys from her pocket once more, she came to a key that was tarnished green, and although it had clearly seen better days, it had a beautifully carved handle with lots of swirls. She pushed the key in and twisted it twice, and it opened outward.

On the other side of the door was another room. At the far end was what appeared to be an altar. A long table draped in a black, velvet cloth with a woven, silver circle donning a pair of horns and a single upside-down cross in its centre. Candles were lit and spread around the cave-like room. The walls were of jagged stone with dark crevices that made perfect shelves for the candles. The room felt cold, and water dripped down the edges of the rock and formed large puddles. As they entered the room, Jenny's icy breath could be seen forming clouds from her barely parted lips. Goosebumps rippled all over her exposed skin, causing her hair to stand on end.

Nora and Lizzie approached the altar and laid Jenny's limp body upon it, arranging small candles and skulls around her. The rest of the girls gathered around, forming a circle around Jenny. It seemed no one noticed two of the girls were missing from the ghoulish pack. Abigail and Sylvie were nowhere to be seen, and as a result of the others not particularly liking them, they went unnoticed.

A hush came over the room and a dark shadow entered the circle of children. The girls all bowed their heads, their gaze meeting the wet stone floor beneath them.

"Praise the Dark Lord and his unholy priest, Tobias Hughes. May they, in partnership, deliver us from this tomb to let our souls walk free. Hail the Dark Lord. Hail Tobias Hughes," the young voices echoed around the room, bouncing off the shiny walls. Once the reverberated voices were silenced, Tobias stepped up to the alter. The flickering glow from the candle's flames made Tobias a little more visible. He stood beside Jenny, his dark figure looming over her in his black robe.

"Tonight, we gain our freedom!" he boomed. Everyone surrounding him broke into applause. The hope they had clung to for years was about to be realised. All they had worked towards, the torture they had been through, it would all come to an end tonight and they would finally be free.

"Tonight, we perform the Familia Sacrificium and the Dark Lord will free us from our cell." Tobias had an evil smirk across his face that was barely visible to those around him. Candlelight twinkled in his monstrous glare.

Lenora stepped up to the altar, bowing her head and kneeling on the cold stone. She held her hand up towards Tobias. She had taken the Dark Lord's book from Jenny's room just before bringing her body down.

"You have done well, my child. The Dark Lord will reward you for your loyalty and devotion." Lenora's eyes met with his and she smiled seductively at him, still convinced they could be together in an unholy afterlife. He took the book from her and reached his other hand out to help Lenora to her feet. After rising, she kissed his knuckles and stepped backward to rejoin the circle.

Tobias placed his cold lips upon the book, kissing it before holding it above his head with both hands.

"Dark Lord, we call upon you to guide us through the rites of Familia Sacrificium. We ask you to grant us the power to exchange souls. A life for a life. So we shall walk free." Tobias had to remember to be careful with his wording. All was not as it appeared.

Tobias placed the book in front of him, between himself and Jenny's body. He noticed that as he did so, Jenny's fingers began to twitch. He knew she could wake at any moment, so he needed to act fast.

He began reading the text before him. "Ego sacrificium ultima heres. Rogo tenebris dominus ad commutationem anima mea enim eius. Sit anima mea licentia hoc carcere, et mandata eius pro."

"I sacrifice my last heir. I pray the Dark Lord to exchange my soul for hers. Let my soul leave this prison and keep hers instead."

"Wait, is he only exchanging for his own soul?" Lizzie whispered to Nora.

"Don't be foolish, he is our saviour, he will release us all."

Tobias let his cloak slip from his body and onto the floor. His body was covered in scars and cuts that still seemed to be oozing in puss. Scars from years of torturing himself in the name of the Dark Lord. Whipping himself, cutting the Dark Lord's name into his flesh. Scars of life now remained with him in death.

In the basin next to the altar, a black substance started to form and swirl as Tobias spoke. The matter was thick and gloopy. It started bubbling as if being heated. Bubbles exploded and the mixture started forming and twisting upwards from the basin. A stench of sulphur oozed from it into the air around them.

"Una anima, quia aliud esse liberum ab inferno in nomine Baltazius Abaddon, fiet!"

"One soul for another to be free from hell. In the name of Baltazius Abaddon, it shall be done!"

"Miss May, he is! What have we done?"

Jenny's eyes were scrolling ferociously beneath her eyelids. Voices imploded inside her ears. Shrieking and shouting. Abigail. Sylvie.

"Wake up! He shall not have you. You may be his heir, but you shall not be his last! Remember *Occidere malum anima*. Live! Wake up!"

Jenny's eyes shot open and she had but mere seconds to react. A dagger dripping in black ooze hung above her. Tobias's eyes were closed as he did a final, internal prayer after dipping the dagger into the ectoplasm-like substance drifting around in the basin. One drop of the repulsive ooze dripped from the sharp point of the blade and onto her chest. Surprisingly, the liquid was cold even though it appeared to be boiling. The coldness struck her, causing her to finally move. She rolled rapidly off the altar, slamming into the concrete ground as she let out a loud shriek.

In an instant, Sylvie and Abigail appeared behind Tobias and struck him with his own dagger whilst he was startled by Jenny's collapse to the ground that interrupted his final prayer.

"No!" he screamed. The black ooze spread throughout his dead body from where the dagger had entered his soul.

"Turns out you can kill a ghost," Sylvie said in shock as she watched the dark substance smother his entire being until he was one big glob of dark ectoplasm.

Jenny grabbed the book and quickly flicked to a page she came across earlier. *Occidere malum anima, To kill an evil soul.* Abigail had said these very words to her whilst she was unconscious on the table. *Had this been her plan all along?*

The text indicated to stab the soul with his own blade and recite the following passage. Jenny climbed to her feet and read so loudly that the spell echoed all around.

"I call upon the Dark Lord. Dico in tenebris, dominus. Banish this soul to your eternal hell. Bannish hoc anima tua aeterna infernum. Forever may he remain in your eternal prison. In aeternum, ut ipse manet in aeternum carcere. In the Dark Lord's name. In tenebris nomen domini. It shall be done. Fiet!"

The black substance that had concealed Tobias erupted and exploded, splattering its dark matter all over the stone walls of the hidden basement. Everyone was on the floor, arms over their heads as though they would be hurt by the evil sludge flying through the air, dead or not. If Jenny was able to kill Tobias once and for all, who knew what would happen if the substance landed on them?

Small eyes started peering over crossed arms, checking to see if it was safe to come back up. The energy that had exploded from within Tobias had sent Jenny flying and her back was bent over the altar so that her torso was resting on the table. All the candles had blown out so no one could see Jenny's body bent in half upon the altar.

Abigail reached up from her crumpled position on the floor and lit one of the candles she had found rolling by her foot. The soft glow extended before them, and she moved her arm around to see the state of the room. The children's souls were still there. Lenora was still there.

"Where's Jenny?" Sylvie asked but then noticed a body on the altar.

"No!" Abigail screamed. "No! I was meant to save you!" She turned and glared at Lenora.

"This was all your fault!" she shouted. "You were so obsessed with him that you didn't see what he was truly up to! You stupid, blind idiot! Thinking he wanted a happily ever after with you! He wanted out of here and was going to do so alone. He was leaving us all here, you stupid old bat! You killed for him, but he wanted nothing to do with you. He hated us just as much in death as he did in life."

EPILOGUE
THE LIGHT AMONGST THE DEAD

"ABIGAIL," A GENTLE VOICE CALLED OUT. Abigail turned around to find Jenny's spirit standing behind her, but she didn't look like the rest of them. She was glowing in a brilliant white light.

"It's okay, Abigail. Tobias is gone, he cannot harm anyone ever again. It ended with me, just as it had to. It's all come to light. I know who I am, I know who you are, and that we are both related to that evil, but in no way are we anything like him. He will rot in the deepest darkest of pits. But you, you get to move on now. It was him that kept you trapped here."

"But it was my fault, I set a curse that was undoable. I didn't know he would be able to trap others here and make them do his bidding. I am so sorry." Sylvie appologised full of regret.

"Sylvie, don't be sorry. That monster put you through hell. He needed stopping and you only did what you could. The most important thing is that it's over. Well, almost." Jenny reached her hand up and a bright white light flowed in from the door.

"Children, it's time for you to move on now. A new life awaits you. There will be no more suffering, no more whippings or torture. Head into the light."

The girls left their positions on the floor and started to walk towards the doorway of light. The glow was so warm and inviting. The first girl to approach the door looked back at Jenny, her eyes glistening in the glow, tears welling up and trickling down her cheeks. "Thank you, Jenny."

The girls went through the door and disappeared into the light. Small giggles and playing were heard through the door, although it wasn't seen. Nora and Lizzie approached the door.

"I don't think so," Jenny said.

The light vanished and in its place was a loud boom. The room shook and the ground cracked. The altar fell into pieces as the ground below it shook violently, and the concrete it sat upon gave way beneath the heavy wood and candles. Flames rushed up out of the hole as the altar and its contents fell into the abyss. Cracks rippled outward to where Lizzie and Nora stood holding one another in fear.

The pair, still huddled together, slowly started backing away from the cracks that reached out toward them, but they could not avoid falling into the depths of hell. A dark, twisting entity seeped out from the hollow and into the air like a black wave reaching toward them. The liquid flowed around them like a hurricane and twisted around them like a rope, holding them together for eternity and dragging their souls into the fiery pit, their screams piercing the air until the ground healed over leaving a sort of dark, burnt scab in its place.

The room was silent. Abigail and Sylvie were still standing with Jenny, and they could not believe what they had just witnessed.

"Is that where Tobias is?" Sylvie asked.

"Sure is. Nora wanted to be with him that much and have children with him and live happily ever after, well now she can. Perhaps not happily, but they're stuck down there all the same, and Lizzie joined them. There was evil in all three of them. Yes, the other girls could have done something about the whole situation and not followed Tobias's orders, but they were brainwashed. Cult leaders do that. He made his school into a cult and brainwashed everyone into doing what he said. The Dark Lord gave him the powers to do so in life and death. Now that the three of them are gone, everyone else can be at peace."

"What about us?" Sylvie asked as she held Abigail's hand.

"The three of us will be on our way too." The light once again glowed around the door, signalling to them it was now their turn. Hand in hand, the three of them walked through the light and into their new lives.

Coming soon from Brianna Raine

When Megan and Ryan move their family from the big city to the rural countryside of Kent, they hoped for a new start full of love and excitement.

Unfortunately for them, Anne-Marie had other ideas.

The eldest daughter Cassie notices strange things happening around the house, her new doll acting strangely and turning up in impossible places. She tries to convince her parents of the strange goings on, but they knew Cassie didn't want to move, and so put all of her 'stories' down to her not wanting to be there.

By the time they realised exactly what was going on, it was too late.

When photographer Adam gets the offer of a lifetime in Peru, him and his friends take full advantage and go for a spiritual experience they will never forget.

Amy is the spiritual one out of the foursome, with her best friend being in fashion and Adam's best mate in computer programming. It's time to forget about their day job's and get closer to the Divine.

But the resort they've booked into isn't the safe haven they believe it to be. A dark practitioner pretending to be a shaman takes advantage of the group, leaving them in the holiday from Hell.

Printed in Great Britain
by Amazon